"ARE YOU LOOKING FOR SOME EXCITEMENT?" DAVID MURMURED.

Maggie's blue eyes narrowed suspiciously. "I'm not sure what you mean."

"I've got an opening for a female companion." His smile was sensuous. "Believe me, the benefits are top-notch."

Maggie bristled at his cold-blooded words, but smiled flirtatiously. "I'm sure your requirements must be very stiff."

"I know what I want: blue eyes, golden hair, a gorgeous smile . . ."

He was leaning down to kiss her, and she quickly slipped out of his reach. "I think I have just the girl for you. Let me give you her number."

David smiled. "Is this your home phone?"

"Oh, no. It's the number of the Wakefield Zoo," she said wickedly. "They've got an orangutan named Kitty who's perfect for you. And I'm sure she's free tonight!"

CANDLELIGHT ECSTASY CLASSIC ROMANCES

WEB OF DESIRE,
Jean Hager

DOUBLE OCCUPANCY,
Elaine Raco Chase

LOVE BEYOND REASON,
Rachel Ryan

MASQUERADE OF LOVE,
Alice Morgan

CANDLELIGHT ECSTASY ROMANCES®

486 THE DRIFTER'S REVENGE, *Kathy Orr*
487 BITTERSWEET TORMENT, *Vanessa Richards*
488 NEVER GIVE IN, *JoAnna Brandon*
489 STOLEN MOMENTS, *Terri Herrington*
490 RESTLESS YEARNING, *Alison Tyler*
491 FUN AND GAMES, *Anna Hudson*

QUANTITY SALES

Most Dell Books are available at special quantity discounts when purchased in bulk by corporations, organizations, and special-interest groups. Custom imprinting or excerpting can also be done to fit special needs. For details write: Dell Publishing Co., Inc., 1 Dag Hammarskjold Plaza, New York, NY 10017, Attn.: Special Sales Dept., or phone: (212) 605-3319.

INDIVIDUAL SALES

Are there any Dell Books you want but cannot find in your local stores? If so, you can order them directly from us. You can get any Dell book in print. Simply include the book's title, author, and ISBN number, if you have it, along with a check or money order (no cash can be accepted) for the full retail price plus 75¢ per copy to cover shipping and handling. Mail to: Dell Readers Service, Dept. FM, P.O. Box 1000, Pine Brook, NJ 07058.

TENDER FURY

Helen Conrad

A CANDLELIGHT ECSTASY ROMANCE®

Published by
Dell Publishing Co., Inc.
1 Dag Hammarskjold Plaza
New York, New York 10017

Copyright © 1987 by Helen Conrad

All rights reserved. No part of this book may be reproduced or transmitted in any form or by any means, electronic or mechanical, including photocopying, recording or by any information storage and retrieval system, without the written permission of the Publisher, except where permitted by law.

Dell ® TM 681510, Dell Publishing Co., Inc.

Candlelight Ecstasy Romance®, 1,203,540, is a registered trademark of Dell Publishing Co., Inc., New York, New York.

ISBN: 0-440-18726-5

Printed in the United States of America

March 1987

10 9 8 7 6 5 4 3 2 1

WFH

To Our Readers:

We have been delighted with your enthusiastic response to Candlelight Ecstasy Romances®, and we thank you for the interest you have shown in this exciting series.

In the upcoming months we will continue to present the distinctive sensuous love stories you have come to expect only from Ecstasy. We look forward to bringing you many more books from your favorite authors and also the very finest work from new authors of contemporary romantic fiction.

As always, we are striving to present the unique, absorbing love stories that you enjoy most—books that are more than ordinary romance. Your suggestions and comments are always welcome. Please write to us at the address below.

          Sincerely,

          The Editors
          Candlelight Romances
          1 Dag Hammarskjold Plaza
          New York, New York 10017

TENDER FURY

CHAPTER ONE

Maggie didn't hear the motorcycle at first. It had been one of those blue funk days that come every now and then, and her mind was filled with grouchy thoughts. She pulled her car into the Youth Center parking lot, switched off the engine and leaned over the steering wheel. Rubbing her hands across her face, she tried to summon a smile for the gymnastics class that was waiting for her on the upper field.

Her hands felt cool over her eyes and she left them there for a moment. She wished—what exactly did she wish for? That she could think of a way to put the running of the Youth Center in the black. That she were married to a wonderful guy and had a house full of bouncing babies. That world peace would come in her time and the rivers would start running chocolate syrup.

She laughed softly, dropping her hands and straightening in her seat. And that was when she heard the scream.

Jumping out of her car, she listened carefully and noticed the whine of a motorcycle coming from the upper field, behind the low, ranch-style office building of the Youth Center.

A sense of alarm raced through her, and she began to feel uneasy about her girls. There were twelve of them, all in their mid-teens, and all waiting for Maggie, who was late, as usual. As she slammed the door of her car, she heard another high-pitched scream, and her heart lept to her throat. Uneasiness turned to fierce protectiveness, and she ran across the parking lot and began to climb the steps to the upper field, taking them two at a time. The motorcycle roared again, and a chorus of screams followed. Maggie ran faster.

From the top of the steps she could see the entire clearing. It was a track set up for jogging, with areas of dirt and sand in the center. Her twelve gymnasts were scattered about in bunches of two and three girls, all jumping up and down and clinging together in excited groups. Zigzagging between them was a huge black motorcycle, its rider dressed in black leather, a hard helmet totally encasing his head.

By now Maggie could see that the screams were really shrieks of delight. The rider revved his bike and pretended to aim at one little knot of girls, making them giggle and jump out of the way, yelping in pretended terror as he passed. Then he turned and aimed at another group. The girls in their pink and lavender tights and leotards made a candy-color contrast to the rider and his shiny black bike.

Maggie knew the girls were in very little danger, but that didn't lessen her fury. Whoever this madman was, he had no business on Youth Center property, and no right to try to impress a bunch of squealing girls with his enormous bike.

She strode out onto the track and stood right in his path, hands on her hips. Her blue-eyed gaze was diamond-hard, and her honey-gold hair cascaded about her shoulders like a lion's mane ruffled by the breeze. The tilt of her chin gave mute testimony to her stubborn nature. She wasn't about to move an inch.

The rider came racing toward her as though he had no time for barricades. She felt her throat tighten a bit as he neared her, but she didn't budge, and he slowed suddenly to avoid a collision. He stopped just inches from her and sat for a moment, unmoving. The engine's roar lowered to a rumble that reminded her of the wary purr of a giant black jungle cat. The rider was still as a statue. Maggie decided she could stare him down if she had to and didn't move a muscle herself but stood, hands still on her hips, glaring at the shiny plastic mask. When he finally lifted a gloved hand to tilt back the shield and reveal his eyes, she felt a tiny thrill of victory.

Two very dark eyes stared out at her. "Hello," a deep voice said. "You got here just in time. I was being overwhelmed by this band of marauding girls." He cocked his head toward the giggling gymnasts, who were edging closer. "I was totally outnumbered, as you can see."

A madman and a wiseacre, all rolled into one.

"The fun's over, mister," Maggie said evenly. "It's time for you to get out of here."

The girls made a murmur of protest. The man shrugged his shoulders slightly and reached down to turn off his engine. When he swung down from the motorcycle and pulled off the helmet, they finally saw what the mystery rider looked like, and Maggie could hear a sigh of appreciation go through the crowd of girls.

Maggie shook her head wearily. She might have known he would be every schoolgirl's dream—wild and dangerous. The very sort to set her students' pulses racing—and Maggie's teeth on edge.

She had to admit he was good-looking. Extremely good-looking. His chin was square and hard, as was his mouth, but his eyes were indefinable as quicksilver—calm yet restless, assured and questioning, cynical yet filled with a sense of hard-edged humor.

His shoulders were wider than he deserved, made even broader by the big leather jacket he wore, while his hips were hard and slim. He was quite intimidating, from the roughly cut line of his jaw to the commanding arrogance of his gaze. His dark eyes were as black as the wavy hair that fell carelessly over his forehead. He was movie-star handsome and then some.

But what surprised her was his age. Instead of the cocky teenager she'd expected, she found herself confronting a full-grown man who was at least five years older than her.

She'd never seen him before. Wakefield was a small town and she'd lived here all her life. She knew just about everyone, at least by sight. But this man was a stranger. They didn't get many strangers here.

"This isn't a motorcycle track," she said when he showed no sign of leaving. She wanted to get rid of him as quickly as possible. "You'll have to go."

His dark eyes glimmered, and she had the distinct impression that he was laughing at her.

"Why don't we take a vote?" he asked slowly, turning toward the girls. "Everyone who wants me to leave, raise your hand."

Not a single hand went up. Maggie glared at her mutinous students.

"Until the Youth Center declares itself an independent nation, I'm in charge here," she announced, pushing her golden hair back with an exasperated gesture and glancing at the arrogant man before her. "What I say goes. And I'm asking you nicely, once and for all, to please get that ugly machine out of here."

"That's *nicely?*" He looked pained. "Now would you expect me to talk about a member of *your* family like that?"

"Family?" She glanced at the shiny bike again, just as he reached out and put a loving hand on the fender.

"The closest I've got."

He was grinning at her, mocking her, and she knew it. There was a sarcastic edge to her voice when she asked, "Brother or sister?"

"Adopted child," he said promptly.

"Really? And here I thought there was such a strong resemblance between you two."

He laughed appreciatively, revealing a dazzling array of white teeth, and she had that uncomfortable feeling again that he was laughing at her, that he could read her mind and identify her weakest point.

Why should she feel that way? He couldn't possibly know her any better than she knew him. And yet the warmth of his gaze as he looked her up and down, the calculated way he seemed to measure her, made her think he knew instinctively what she was feeling.

She shook her head, breaking away from his glance and looking toward the Sierras in the distance as though to gather strength from the mountains. Something about him really annoyed her. "Would you please just pack up your macho toy and go home?" she demanded.

"Sorry," he said calmly. "I can't do that."

She narrowed her blue eyes. "Yes, you can." She spoke slowly and distinctly, as though to a child. "All you have to do is get back on that thing and turn it in the right direction. I'll give you a push if I have to, to get you going. It's all downhill after that."

His mouth twitched, as though he were holding back a smile. He began tugging at the fingers of one glove, pulling it off his hand. "You're a toughy, aren't you?" he said softly. "How does a lady who looks so soft get to be so tough?"

She'd never been accused of that before. Strict, yes. The girls were always complaining about the pace she set for them and the rules she enforced. But tough?

The girls were no help. They'd crowded in close now and were giggling and talking behind their hands in loud stage whispers. They thought this motorcycle maniac was gorgeous and they were letting him know it. He tossed them a grin, as though he were on their side.

"Girls, get over to the sand pit where we do our calisthenics," Maggie ordered. "Randi, you lead them in the first two sets."

There was grumbling, but they were used to doing what Maggie told them to do. She watched as they began to straggle reluctantly toward the sand pit, scuffing their running shoes in the dirt and casting envious glances back at Maggie. When they finally reached the sand pit, she turned back to the tall man standing before her. He'd said she looked soft.

"Looks can be deceiving," she snapped. "I'll bet you're living proof of that."

She'd meant a variation on the old saw of Pretty is as pretty does, but the way he laughed, she had a feeling he read more into her simple attack than she'd meant.

"You're probably right," he agreed, pulling off his other glove. "So I hope you're not jumping to any conclusions."

She wasn't sure what conclusions he was talking about. She saw before her a mature man who still played teenagers' games, as far as she was concerned. He was awfully handsome, but other than that there couldn't be much to recommend him. Yet even as she told herself those things, she felt something quiver inside her, as if she were traitorously pleased with the warmth of his dark eyes and the strong, square line of his hands. They looked like hands that could do anything—fix a motorcycle, soothe a baby, touch a woman so that she . . .

Maggie swallowed hard to thrust back the picture that had come unbidden to her mind. She wasn't going to let herself get silly here. It wasn't in her nature to respond to a man in such a primitive way.

"My conclusions aren't very relevant," she said, cursing the huskiness she heard in her own voice. "It's time for you to leave."

One dark eyebrow arched. "What's your name, tough

lady?" he asked in an intimate tone that made her tremble.

The man's arrogance never quit! If only he weren't so damn good-looking. "My name is none of your business," Maggie snapped, wishing she could think of a better put-down to silence him. "Now please get on your bike and get out of here."

But instead of doing as she ordered, he stuffed his gloves into the pocket of his jacket and took a step closer to her. When she looked up into his eyes, with alarm, something caught and held her. It must have lasted for only a second or two, but it seemed to go on forever. He hadn't reached out to touch her, but she felt like he had. It was as though something in his dark eyes had beckoned to her, pulled her to him, and now she was shaken and unsteady. She held out her hand to regain her balance, and he took it in his.

The contact with his warm hand startled her and she quickly shook off the dizzy feeling. Yanking her hand away, she stepped back, flushing with embarrassment.

"Please go," she whispered just a little shakily. At that moment a shout came from the stairway.

"Mr. Duke," was the call. "Glad you could make it."

They both turned to see Burt, the Youth Center director, hurrying toward them.

"I see you've met," Burt said as he neared them. "But just in case you haven't introduced yourselves, David Duke, meet Maggie Jones, my right-hand woman." He smiled at them both. "Maggie, David here has agreed to give the Winners a bike-riding exhibition this afternoon. I told him he could come up to the track and use the center area for some practicing. I guess I forgot that you bring your gym class up here for a warm-up every day."

Maggie looked up into the rider's eyes, her own gaze bright with accusation, but she could see from his grin that he felt no remorse for letting her think all this time that he was a trespasser.

"I'm afraid I've disrupted the gymnastics warm-up," David said, though he didn't sound a bit sorry. He smiled down at Maggie. "What can I do to make it up to you?"

Disappear from my life, Maggie thought irritably. And she might have said it if Burt hadn't been standing right there. She avoided David's gaze. "I wish you'd told me," she said to Burt. "I'd have had the girls meet me in the gym instead."

The gym was where most of the sports activities took place. Right now the Youth Center was running a basketball clinic, an elementary level football league, swimming lessons of every sort and aerobic dancing, as well as the after-school gymnastics program. And then there was the Winners Club, Burt's special baby. The Winners was a club for boys from troubled homes and disadvantaged backgrounds, many of whom had been in minor scrapes with the law. And all of them were ripe for redemption, according to Burt.

"This just came up today," Burt told her apologetically. "I've been looking for someone to teach the Winners something about dirt bikes, and when I heard David Duke had moved to our town, I was so excited, I called him right away—"

"Gave me the old strong arm," David inserted with a grin. "And here I am."

"I suppose you're some kind of expert or something," Maggie said, knowing as she spoke that her tone was accusing rather than respectful.

He nodded, as though he regretted it as much as she did. "I'm afraid so."

"Trials Champ in the Western States Championship last month in Colorado," Burt announced happily. "The boys are thrilled."

Maggie had to smile. It looked to her like Burt was the one who was thrilled. He was a middle-aged man, slightly balding and more than a little overweight, with a heart as big as forever. He ran the Youth Center on a grant from the city council, along with whatever funds he could raise by hook or by crook and whatever volunteer assistance he could roust from the community. Training children to have bodies as strong and healthy as possible was a passion with him. Maggie had worked for him for four years and she adored him. She'd come out of college with a degree in history and a minor in physical education. She'd thought she'd be a teacher, but there weren't many openings in Wakefield, the small town outside of Visalia, California, where she'd lived all her life. So she'd taken a provisional job with Burt, just helping out in the afternoons. Within two months she'd come on full-time as his administrative assistant, and by now she was in charge of almost as many programs as he was. Teaching jobs had opened elsewhere and she'd ignored them. She'd found her niche.

"Let your girls stay and watch," Burt urged. "Who knows, they might want to take up the sport."

Maggie grinned. Except for Randi Farlow, who would

probably dare to try anything, most of her girls this season were the china-doll type, more concerned with how they looked in their leotards than how well they could execute a balance beam routine.

"I'll see if they want to stay," she promised Burt.

"Great." He glowed with enthusiasm. "I'll go down and see what's keeping the boys." He hurried off toward the stairs.

"Well, I guess it's about time for me to get to work," David said lazily, pulling on his gloves again. She watched as he swung a long leg across the seat of the motorcycle. Once he'd settled himself, he held his helmet before him and looked up at her hopefully. "I don't suppose you'd want to give me a kiss for luck?"

For some reason his words took her breath away, and she had to force herself to speak normally. "No," she managed to murmur, "not really."

He sighed. "I was afraid of that. And you look so damn kissable, too." He grinned when he saw the outrage in her eyes, then pulled on the helmet, kicked the engine to life and rode into the center of the field.

The motorcycle gave a roar, and David began his exhibition. Maggie walked over to stand near her girls, watching. She noticed for the first time that rocks and barrels had been set up in the center of the track. Instead of racing up and down as she'd expected, David was taking the motorcycle very slowly, weaving it in and out and over the barriers much like a show horse performed dressage.

"It's called trials riding," Burt said, coming over to stand near her for a moment, once he'd gotten his boys in place. "In competition he would have a set course to follow, very difficult. He's supposed to ride and keep perfect balance without touching his feet to the ground. Every time he has to use a foot to steady himself, he loses a point."

She hadn't seen him use a foot yet as he led his bike slowly, smoothly around seemingly impossible obstacles. She realized that what he was doing was a feat of skill, not brute strength.

Burt went back to the boys, who seemed awed by David's performance. The girls were affected, too, but not as much by the riding as by other attributes of the man.

"Oh, wow." Randi sighed, gazing at David dreamily. "Isn't he a fox?"

"More like a wolf," Maggie muttered to herself. Still, she was impressed by the show he was putting on. He wasn't only an attractive man, he could ride, too.

The girls gasped and she looked at the rider again, watching as he finessed his bike up and over a boulder by what looked to be sheer willpower. He could handle the shiny black machine like a trainer with a tiger, coaxing and maneuvering, outsmarting the obstacles. Even though she knew nothing about the finer points of what he was doing, it was beautiful to watch. He seemed to know all about his bike, to know exactly what to do to make it purr.

Did he handle women with the same mastery? She suspected that he did, and the thought made her breath catch in her throat. When she realized that her heart was pounding uncontrollably, she knew it was time to leave.

"Let's go, girls," she said, ignoring their cries of distress. David was ending his exhibition, and the boys were crowding around him, but Maggie led the girls quickly off the field. "We've got a lot of work to do," she said shortly in answer to their complaints. "We've wasted enough time already."

As they left the field, she was tempted to look back one last time, but she steeled herself and didn't do it. As she understood it, David Duke had come to the Youth Center as a one-time favor. With any luck, she might never see him again.

There wasn't much of a downtown area to the little town of Wakefield, but what there was sparkled. Small shops stood side by side along a street lined with olive trees. Maggie and her long-time friend Cathy Wilson were window-shopping in the cool autumn twilight after sharing a three-layer monte cristo sandwich at Laverne's Tea Room.

Cathy was waving her short, plump arms in exasperation while Maggie lingered over the new display in the jeweler's window.

"Come on, Maggie," the dynamic redhead urged. "Tell me what happened. You've spent the whole evening complaining about this Hell's Angel who disrupted your gymnastics class—"

Maggie turned back to walk with her friend. The street lamps were coming on, giving the street a warm glow. It was fall in the San Joaquin Valley. Someone in a nearby neighborhood was burning leaves, and the scent was in the air. Maggie took a deep breath and held it, loving the wonderful smell of fall. Then her mind drifted back to what Cathy was saying.

"He wasn't actually a Hell's Angel," she said calmly.

Cathy rolled her eyes. "Well, greasy motorcycle slob—"

"Oh no, he wasn't a bit greasy," she said quickly.

Cathy made a face. "Then just exactly what was your complaint, my darling friend?"

Maggie turned away and found herself staring into the bridal shop window at a lovely lace wedding gown. "It was his attitude," she said softly, staring at the rhinestone-studded tiara the mannequin wore.

Cathy shook her head. "Okay, bad attitude. I hope you never run into the character again." She moved impatiently. "Forget the motorcycle dude. What I really want to know is, what happened when you talked to Bill?"

Maggie stopped in front of the bookstore and gazed in at the best sellers all lined up in a row. "I told Bill to give me some time to think about it," she said softly.

"Think about it?" Cathy's red curls fairly bristled. *"Think about it?* Why didn't you just plain tell him to get his carcass out of your life? Get lost?"

Maggie sighed. "Because, Cathy, I don't want him to get lost. I've told you a million times."

"You've told me, all right. But I refuse to listen." Cathy snorted. "Can't you see Bill's not right for you?"

"No," Maggie retorted calmly. "I don't see that at all. In fact, he's perfect for me. Everything I've always wanted."

"And less," Cathy grumbled, but Maggie didn't listen.

She'd always had a very clear picture in her mind of

22

the man she would marry. Someone steady and reliable and calm, but gracious and loving. Pat Boone could have played the role. She'd waited, but the perfect man hadn't come along. There was a hole in her life, a void where that man should be. She'd always assumed she would marry and have children. From the time she was a little girl playing with baby dolls, she knew she wanted a home and family more than anything else in the world. Not that she didn't want a career as well, but she needed more.

There'd been no doubts about finding the perfect man at first. She'd cruised through high school dating one boy after another, then had gone steady with a few different boys in college. But there'd been no one really special. She just kept waiting, confident that he was just around the corner.

And then suddenly college was over and she was back home and it hadn't happened. She dated, all right, but there was never any magic, never any violins.

Lately she'd been seeing Bill Smith. Come to think of it, Bill looked a lot like Pat Boone. She stifled a quick grin. When she'd first met him, she'd known right away that he was the solution to all her problems. He was perfect. They got along fine; her parents adored him. If only there was a little more magic . . .

"Face it, Cathy," Maggie said, sinking down onto a stone bench on the side of the street. "He's perfect for me. What am I waiting for? I don't have forever. If I want a home and family—"

"If you're so hot to exercise your maternal instincts, I'll buy you a baby doll," Cathy snapped. "But I will not allow you to marry this oh-so-nice but oh-so-boring individual just because you feel like making a nest." She shook her head. "You and your brother. What am I going to do with the two of you?"

Maggie laughed softly. "Mark's all right. He's just a little serious—"

"A little serious! That's an understatement. And lately he growls every time he sees me coming."

Maggie giggled. "You can hardly blame him. After all, that birthday present you gave him last month was not really to his taste—and you knew it wouldn't be."

Cathy pretended bewilderment. "See-through black nylon underwear? Every man I know has a pair."

"Not Mark."

Cathy looked smug. "He does now."

"No he doesn't. He threw them out the very next morning."

Cathy's face fell. "Someone has to wake that man up to the twentieth century. He's such a stick-in-the-mud."

Maggie's eyes danced. "That's a crusade you took on in junior high and you still haven't given up. Why do you bother to keep trying to push him into a century he doesn't belong in?"

Cathy threw her hands up. "Every human being is worth saving, even Mark. He flounders out there in the Sea of Boredom and I keep throwing him life preservers. One of these days he's going to grab hold of one of them and I'll pull him up to join the rest of us."

A loud sound from the street suddenly caught Maggie's attention, and she looked up. Her eyes widened, and she grabbed Cathy's arm.

"Look! There he is. The guy on the motorcycle."

Cathy stood and watched as he rode past, while Maggie shrank back into the shadows of the plants. "Ooooh," Cathy said as he passed. "Yes, I see what you mean. Cute buns."

"Cathy!" Maggie pulled at her skirt to get her back on the bench.

"Well, he does have cute buns. And that's about all I can see of him with all that leather on." Cathy turned to watch him again as he rode around the corner and out of sight. "If he shakes you up this much," she said musingly, "I say, go for him."

Maggie's mouth dropped. "What on earth are you talking about?"

Cathy's green eyes were suddenly penetratingly perceptive. "You wouldn't have been bending my ear about this guy all evening if there wasn't some 'go for it' involved."

Maggie was flustered. "I'm not going to do any such thing!"

"Why not?" Cathy grinned. "Anything to rescue you from Bill the Pill."

Maggie rose and started off down the street in the opposite direction from where David Duke had disappeared. Cathy came running after her, but Maggie refused to talk about the motorcyclist any more.

Not that Maggie forgot him. Indeed, she was plagued with worries the rest of the evening. Should she settle for what was right and proper, she wondered, or should she hold out for the magic she'd been missing for so long? Should she marry Bill Smith? she asked herself as she slipped under the bedcovers later that night. And if not, why not?

"Maggie Jones, do you claim to have any valid reason to turn the man down?" she asked herself.

No. Not a one. Especially not one that had anything to do with wild motorcycle riders who could put tread marks on a woman's heart with no effort at all.

CHAPTER TWO

"You are elected."

Maggie sank into the swivel chair behind her desk in the Youth Center administrative offices. Everything seemed to be going against her these days. "That's hardly fair," she complained weakly. "I didn't get to vote."

"There were only two votes in this election," Burt told her smugly. "And they were both mine."

He thought he was being cute. If only he knew how much she hated his idea. "I really don't think I should be the one to do it . . ." she started hesitantly.

"Of course you're the one," Burt countered heartily. "You've been saying you wanted to get into the recruiting side of this business. Here's your chance."

Had she ever really said that? "But I don't know a thing about motorcycles or dirt riding or any of that. How can I convince David Duke we need him to set up a program if I don't even know what sort of things we need?"

Burt dismissed her argument with a wave of his hand. "He'll know all that himself. I've already gone over the type of program I have in mind with him."

She turned to look at her boss. "And he turned you down."

"Yup."

She sighed. "Just what makes you think *I* can persuade him to change his mind?"

He threw her a baleful glance. "Come on, Maggie. I saw the way he was looking at you."

She drew herself up with indignation. "You're not suggesting—!"

"That you use your body as barter?" He grinned at her. "Of course not, that's not what I mean at all. I just noticed that he thought you were pretty nice to look at. I thought a little feminine persuasion might do the trick."

She was still glaring at him. "You don't want me to cry into a handkerchief, do you?" she asked accusingly.

"No."

"Then if I'm not supposed to use my body, or my tears," she said in a last-ditch effort to get him to change his mind, "just what is my female advantage supposed to be?"

Burt had had his fill of her arguments. "He liked you," he told her shortly. "It's your job to turn that like into a desire to help our boys."

"Our boys" meant his Winners Club. He had it in his head that learning how to handle a motorcycle properly was the only thing that was going to save them. "They relate to this stuff," he told her. "They like the sports okay, but some of them aren't natural athletes and they need a motivator, something to improve their attitude. They went crazy over David yesterday. If we get them involved in dirt-bike riding, they'll have something to do with their time besides hanging out and getting in trouble."

He really cared so much, and he was so sure that this would do the trick. "All right," she said grudgingly. "I'll do my best."

"Attagirl," he said bracingly. "Tell him how much it will mean to the community. He's just moved here to Wakefield. Convince him this will be a great way to meet new people."

Maggie had to smile. Somehow she didn't think meeting people would ever be a problem with David Duke. He probably had to beat them off with a stick.

"And tell him we need him by this weekend," Burt added. "I've got a local motorcycle dealer who's promised to donate three bikes. If David doesn't show, no one will know what to do with them."

She watched him leave her office, then slumped in her chair. She'd hoped she would never have to see David again. The man was entirely too arrogant for her taste, and incredibly irritating on top of that. She didn't relish having to smile and coax him into doing what Burt wanted.

Nevertheless, she had to do it. Rousing herself with a sigh, she began to plan her strategy. If she had to do it, she wanted to do it well. Burt deserved as much.

A little over an hour later Maggie drove her little car into the parking lot at Farlow Electronics for her confrontation with David Duke. The building was a large granite structure with a huge lawn rolling out in all directions. Farlow was the most important employer in Wakefield, and though many of the residents worked in nearby Visalia and some even as far away as Fresno, most of the townspeople worked for local service firms or Farlow Electronics.

Still she'd been surprised when Burt had given her this as David's business address. Her brother Mark worked for the same company as a scientific programmer. She couldn't imagine what David might do there. She wouldn't have supposed Farlow to have much use for expert motorcycle riding.

Maggie paused at the giant glass doorway, trying to prepare herself for the task she was about to perform. This time when she saw David she wasn't going to fall for his lively charm. This time she was going to keep her head about her. She only hoped she could do that and still convince him to start the riding program at the Youth Center.

"Hi, Maggie," the receptionist said, recognizing her. "Are you visiting Mark? I'm afraid you'll have to go through security."

"Actually, Cassie, I'm here to see David Duke," she said with a friendly smile. "The champion motorcycle rider."

"Motorcycles!" Cassie crowed. "Does he do that too?"

Maggie blinked at her. She hadn't expected Cassie to know who she was talking about, but apparently she was all too familiar with David. But of course. He was so handsome, probably every woman in the place knew him by name, even though he'd only just started working there.

I'll bet he's got an ego the size of the Goodyear blimp,

Maggie said to herself as she made her way down the hall. Just the sort of man she hated. For just a moment she closed her eyes and wished she could turn around, march back to the Y and tell Burt she just couldn't do it.

While Maggie was going through security, filling out forms and making promises not to spy, David was staring out the window of his office, wondering how he'd managed to land himself in such a dull hick town. Despite the motorcycles, he was a city boy at heart, used to flash and excitement. All of which were in woefully short supply in Wakefield.

His intercom rang and he turned to his desk, grateful for any diversion at the moment.

"Yes, Sheila?"

"You've got a call from Willie Jacobs on line two."

"Thanks." Willie Jacobs. David hadn't seen him since the Nationals last spring. Flicking the call onto his speaker, he leaned back in his chair and propped up his feet on the desk.

"Hey, Willie," he said. "How's it going?"

"David Duke, old man." His friend's country twang filled the room. "What the hell are you doing in that little oil spot of a town?"

David laughed. "Work, Willie. Making a living. You've heard of that before."

"I've heard of it, boy. I just never gave it a try myself. Been too busy eating dirt and polishing chrome."

"Are you here in town?"

"Nope. Passing through Fresno and thought I'd give

you a call. Won't have time to drop by on this run. Maybe next time."

"Too bad." David sighed. "But listen, partner, you grew up in small towns. Give me some advice. So far it's been one long snooze around here. What can I do for excitement?"

"That's an easy one, boy. There's only one interesting thing to do in a town that size. You gotta seduce the local virgin."

David laughed. He noticed that Mark, a fellow computer programmer, had appeared in his doorway. Apparently Mark had heard Willie's suggestion, and his face registered shock at Willie's idea of a joke. David waved him to come in and take a seat. He continued with his conversation, though the speaker phone made it clearly audible to anyone in the room.

"I take it you speak from experience," he needled Willie.

"Course. There's nothing like it."

"Just tell me this, good buddy. How can you tell who the virgin is?"

"That's easy. You start with the librarian and then work your way through the schoolteachers, keeping an eye out for the blushers. You won't have any problem once you get into it." His laugh was suggestive. "You might even find the process of elimination the best part of the whole deal."

David laughed along with him. "Thanks for the tip, Willie," he said, not noticing Mark's disapproving frown.

"On the other hand," Willie went on, "if you're in a

hurry, you could just pick up the next woman who walks through your doorway. It's all a matter of timing."

David laughed again, exchanged a few pleasantries with his old friend, then rang off. When he looked up, Mark was gone.

Meanwhile Maggie, finished with security, was surprised to be directed toward the same floor where her brother's office was.

"Third door on the right," she was told.

That was only two doors away from her brother's office. Could David Duke really be a computer programmer, just like her serious brother Mark? Impossible!

The third door to the right was ajar, so Maggie peeked into the office. The chair was turned away from her, but she recognized the black hair she could see above the back of it.

"Mr. Duke?" she asked hesitantly.

The chair turned and David was on his feet immediately. For one long moment she stared at him, not entirely sure this was the same man she'd met the previous afternoon.

The eyes were the same, and so was the good-looking face. But this man was dressed in an Italian suit so well cut, brain surgeons might have had a hand in it. The starched white collar of his shirt made a startling contrast to the smooth tan of his skin and the midnight black of his hair. His tie was just right, and there was a gold pin holding it in place at the collar. He looked like something out of *Gentleman's Quarterly*. There wasn't a hint of the biker to be seen.

She could hardly believe her eyes. "Don't jump to conclusions," he'd told her yesterday, but she'd gone ahead and made the leap anyway. Now she had to get back across that gorge, and the drop was breathtaking.

"David Duke?" she asked, staring up into his laughing eyes. "The real David Duke?"

"None other." Taking her hand, he began to lead her into the office.

"You're sure?" she asked, only half-joking. "You're not really his twin brother, are you?"

"Dudley Duke?" he murmured mockingly. "Or maybe the ubiquitous Dwight?"

"No," she breathed, sinking into a chair across from his desk, still marveling at the elegant portrait he made. "More like Drake or Damien."

He chuckled and threw himself down into the swivel chair. "Come on, Maggie. I'm still the same lovable biker you met yesterday. Clothes don't make the man, you know."

She pursed her lips. Proverbs sounded out of place coming from him.

She had to admit, though, he'd thrown her off balance. She'd been prepared to play defense against a rough-and-ready offense, but instead she was face to face with finesse.

She wouldn't act cold, she decided, because that would make her look as though she were scared of him. If he wanted to tease, she would tease right back. He wanted proverbs? She had a full supply. "You can't judge a book by its cover," she agreed, tongue in cheek.

"True." He nodded wisely. Eyes bright, he shook a

finger at her. "But you've also got to remember, you can't make a silk purse out of a sow's ear."

She felt a smile tugging at her wide mouth. "That suit is silk, isn't it?" she asked, her voice husky with laughter.

"Absolutely," he replied with a straight face, picking an imaginary bit of lint from his sleeve.

"Well, I guess that proves it," she said. He actually made her want to laugh. She'd never dreamed she would begin her interview with him like this.

"Proves what?" he challenged, but she wasn't about to be cornered into taking anything seriously.

"Pretty is as pretty does, of course," she announced triumphantly. "Everyone knows that."

"Of course." He hit his forehead with the palm of his hand. "How could I have forgotten?"

"I don't know. Just lucky, I guess."

Despite all her best intentions, she met his grin with one of her own, and felt something melting inside. She'd come to conquer him, and instead he'd tangled her up in silliness. She straightened her shoulders, trying to get back on the track.

"Let me guess why you're here," he said suddenly, leaning across the desk toward her. "I'll bet it has something to do with dirt tracks and teenage boys."

She hesitated. He wasn't even going to let her use her well-rehearsed lead-in. "Something like that," she admitted reluctantly.

"Much as I'd like to hear your sales pitch, I'll save you the trouble. I'm not going to do it."

She took a deep breath. "But Mr. Duke, you don't even know—"

"Mr. Duke?" He raised a dark eyebrow.

She dropped her eyes. "D-David," she murmured, wondering why on earth it was so difficult to say his name to his face. "I don't think you understand how important this is. These boys need someone—"

"I know." He rose abruptly and walked to the window, looking out at the green hills on the horizon. When he spoke again, his voice was rough with something that sounded close to anger. "I know a lot better than you could ever guess. And if you knew more about me, more about my past, you wouldn't even bother to ask." He hesitated. "You're the one who doesn't understand."

He stood very still, his back to her, and she waited, wondering what his reasons were, why his voice had grown so cold and hard. "I'll never understand if you don't tell me," she said at last.

His eyes darkened. Telling her about his background, his childhood, the forces that had made him the man he was, was out of the question. He'd never told anyone, and he supposed he never would.

When he turned back his eyes were guarded. "I just don't have the time," he said evenly.

Maggie looked at him steadily. "I see," she said slowly. "I suppose you have a family to think of."

"No." He shook his head. That was the last thing that would ever tie him down. "No family. Except for my bikes, of course." He smiled slightly.

"Then you must be involved with practicing and competition—"

"No." He leaned back against the corner of his desk. "That's not the sort of time I'm talking about. What I mean is, I won't be here long enough to get involved in community projects."

She gazed at him uncertainly.

"I'm a consultant," he said, regaining some of his old smoothness. "I come into a company, fix up the problems and go on to the next place. I was in Chicago before this and I've got an offer for Saudi Arabia next."

"Saudi Arabia?" she repeated, eyes wide.

"Or Sao Paulo, Brazil. I haven't decided which one it will be." He shrugged his shoulders. "My average stay is six months. The longest I've worked in any one place was nine months in Florida, when they were putting in Disney World."

"I see."

"Do you?" He said it softly and she frowned, hearing something ambiguous in the simple question. His dark eyes were studying her boldly. If his aim was to keep her off balance, she had to admit he was doing just fine. Her gaze wavered, making it difficult to sustain any sort of defiant front.

"Where do you call home?" she asked, as much to get him talking again as to have the answer.

"Home?" His grin was slow and impudent. "Home is where I hang my hat. Or helmet, as the case happens to be."

He seemed so nonchalant, so uncaring. Footloose and fancy free. She couldn't imagine living that way.

Still, she hadn't come to get to know him better. She had a job to do here. "Well, six months is long enough to get a program going," she suggested. "With the basics set up, maybe someone else would be willing to take over when you left."

"No." His dark eyes were suddenly cool. "The answer is no, and it's not going to change. I gave the exhibition yesterday, but I'm not going to do any more."

She stared at him and a tiny flame of anger flickered within her. He was making excuses and she knew it. He could make the time if he wanted to. She thought of Burt, who gave one thousand percent, and of those pathetically arrogant boys who needed a chance, and suddenly she was angry. David Duke had no family. He had no network of friends here. Why didn't he have time to give a couple of hours a week in hopes of saving a few unlucky boys from a useless life?

She knew she had no right to be angry. After all, if the man didn't want to do it, he didn't have to. Ordinarily she would have shrugged it off. But somehow she couldn't with David. Suddenly she cared very much whether he did it or not. There had to be some way to persuade him to overcome this selfish attitude. She just hadn't thought of it yet.

She glanced around the office, looking for a clue. "You aren't really a computer programmer, are you?" she asked skeptically, though the evidence was right before her.

He looked at the work piled high on his desk. "I thought I was," he said, pretending surprise. "Do you have information to the contrary?"

She shook her head. "No, but I know a lot of programmers. And none of them is like you at all."

He shook his head. "There you go, jumping to conclusions again. I'm a programmer, all right. I love the work. It's like spending your days doing puzzles or reading mysteries and figuring out who done it."

"Mind games," she murmured.

"Exactly." He smiled at her. "But it doesn't consume my life. I love motorcycles, too. And other recreational activities."

She ignored the implications of his last statement and hurriedly asked, "And you wouldn't enjoy teaching a bunch of eager kids to love bikes, too? A new generation?"

He looked almost startled by the concept. "No."

"You're a taker, is that it?" she asked softly, watching his reaction. "You want to grab for all *you* can get and to hell with the rest of us."

His brows drew together. "Hey, listen—"

"That's the way it looks to me." Her tone was steady, but there was fury boiling beneath the surface. "You have a chance to do something really worthwhile here, something that would hardly inconvenience you at all. And you'd rather have your precious freedom." She glared at him angrily. "I think you're greedy and selfish."

"Listen, lady," he said menacingly, his face hard and cold. "If I'm greedy and selfish, it's to make up for things I didn't get in the past. Okay? I learned early that it's every man for himself. I've got my own life, the way I like it, and no one's going to tamper with it."

They glared at one another for a long, tense moment. Maggie felt frustration surge like a sob in her throat, and she bit her lip to hold it back. Damn him! How had he conjured this rush of emotion in her? She was usually so cool and controlled. Slowly, determinedly, she swallowed and eased herself back in the chair, forcing herself to be calm.

"So you won't do it," she said softly at last.

His face softened, too, looking relieved, as though he thought she were finally backing down and was glad to get this roadblock out of the way. "No. And that's my final word on the subject."

He watched her for a moment, and a speculative gleam slowly appeared in his eyes. His gaze slipped over her golden hair, strewn with silvery lights from the sunshine that spilled in through his window. Soft hair. Warm—if wary—face . . .

Suddenly he thought of his telephone conversation with Willie. Maggie had certainly been the next woman to walk through his door. He wondered if she blushed.

"How about you?" he asked softly, hoping she was ready to go back to the boy-girl playfulness they'd started with. "Are you looking for something to do?"

Maggie narrowed her crystal-blue gaze as though preparing to ward something off. "I'm not sure I know what you mean," she hedged uneasily.

Nevertheless her gaze strayed down over his body and lingered on the fine fabric of his suit hugging his muscular thighs. Suddenly she was finding it hard to breathe, and she forced herself to look away. Catching sight of David's face, she saw that his eyes were gleaming with laughter. She was sure he knew exactly what she'd been looking at and exactly what she'd been feeling. Warmth flooded her cheeks and she looked away quickly, cursing herself for being so easy to read, cursing him for being so damn impertinent, even if only with his eyes.

"I've got an opening of my own I'm looking to fill," he said before she had a chance to tell him off. "A short-term job that needs doing."

She took a deep breath and held back the sharp retort that rose in her throat. He was teasing again. She might as well play along. The oaf didn't even realize she was still angry. "Is that right?" she said, raising her chin. "And what might that be?"

He leaned back and watched her from beneath lowered lids. "I've got an opening for a female companion, right now. The benefits are top-notch."

She bit her lip, wanting to tell him just what he could do with his phony "job." But then she stopped herself. After all, he probably was half-serious. He'd only been in town for a week, and he seemed to be a man who liked to have a woman around. There was something cold-blooded about his putting it in terms of hiring her for a position, even if he was only playing with her.

Two could play as well as one. Getting her emotions under control, she fluttered her eyelashes flirtatiously and gazed up at him. "Then I'm sure the requirements are pretty stiff. I don't imagine just any woman could make the grade."

He seemed to relax before her very eyes, and she could almost hear him say, "This is more like it. This is the way a woman *ought* to act."

But he didn't say that aloud. Instead he said, "That's right. Only qualified applicants need apply." He smiled, all suave seduction. "You want to leave your number?"

41

Her smile was strained. "Don't call us, we'll call you?" she asked. What an ego this man had! She tilted her head coyly. "And just what are the requirements for this marvelous position?"

He was moving toward her slowly. "They're pretty specific," he murmured in a low, husky voice, reaching out to touch the wispy ends of her hair. "Blue eyes are an absolute necessity." His hand slid down and gently touched her chin, raising her face toward his. "Other essentials are golden hair, a gorgeous smile and a dimple" —he touched his finger to her cheek—"right there."

He was leaning down, and she knew that if she didn't move, he would kiss her. To her horror, the thought made her pulse race. But the flame of anger still burned, and she forced herself to slip out of her chair just before his lips touched hers. "I think I might have just the girl for you," she said pertly, moving out of his reach.

"Do you?" He was moving toward her again, so sure of himself, so certain that she would want what he had to offer. "I thought you might."

She turned toward the desk just before he reached her, picking up a pencil and a stray piece of paper. "Here, I'll give you her number," she said hastily, jotting it down. "Why don't you give her a call?"

She started toward the door of the office. David picked up the paper and looked at it, slightly puzzled. "Is this your home phone?"

"Oh no," she said from the doorway. "It's the number of the Wakefield Zoo. They've got an orangutan named Kitty who'll be perfect for you." Her grin was horizon wide as she watched his face change. Then she took off down the hall, followed only by his shout of laughter.

She pounded on the elevator button, but it seemed to take a lifetime in coming. When the doors crept slowly open, she hurried in and looked back down the hall. David was just rounding the corner as the doors closed.

She took a giant breath and let it out again. She hadn't felt this good in ages! She wanted to let out a whoop of triumph, but she glanced at the other woman sharing the elevator and held it back.

The elevator reached the main floor and the doors slid silently open. And there was David, waiting to meet her.

"Oh no," Maggie cried in exasperation. "How did you do that?"

He shrugged. "I took the stairs."

"But even so—"

He took her elbow and began leading her from the building. "I slid down the banister," he admitted. "And believe me, it's not as much fun as it was when I was a kid."

She tried to choke back the laugh but it was no use. He was without a doubt the most impossible man she'd ever met.

"Where do you think you're taking me?" she asked as they strolled out to the parking lot. "I don't need an escort to my car."

"It's lunchtime," he said, pulling her a little closer. "I'm taking you out to lunch."

"Oh, are you really?" Her tone was indignant. She tried to pull away from him, but he wasn't letting her go. "I didn't hear your invitation."

"Probably not," he said. "You were too busy thinking of ways to trip me up."

She couldn't help a self-satisfied smile. "You deserved it."

"You're right. And to make up for it, I'm taking you to lunch."

No you're not, she told herself firmly. *Not in a million years.*

But she couldn't seem to say it out loud. She looked at him speculatively—at his easy grin, his handsome face. Maybe, just maybe, she could talk him into volunteering to help Burt if she went with him. "Oh, all right," she said, trying to frown so he wouldn't think he'd won anything. She glanced down at the cream-color linen slacks and blue cotton sweater she was wearing. "Where are we going?" she asked. "Am I dressed all right?"

His chuckle should have warned her. "Don't worry about a thing. You look beautiful."

He stopped in front of a red motorcycle. "Here we are."

She gaped at it. "Don't you have a car?"

"Of course. Well, a van, actually. I need one to pull the trailer I use to haul my three motorcycles. But for regular transportation I use this." He waved a hand toward the street bike. "You're going to love it."

That was doubtful. Extremely doubtful. She'd never been on a motorcycle before and she'd never had the slightest desire to.

"We could go in my car," she suggested hopefully.

"Not a chance." He pulled the helmet from the back of the bike and began to slip it over her head. "You're going to wear this and I'm going to drive very carefully and you're going to love it."

She took a step backward, but it was too late.

"Not scared, are you?" he taunted, fastening the strap around her head.

Her fighting instinct surfaced. "Of course not!" she snapped.

But then she looked at the big ugly machine she was expected to ride, and her heart was in her throat.

She glanced at David, who was watching her, waiting. She felt like an idiot with the enormous helmet on her head, but at least the shield covered her eyes. Maybe he couldn't tell how frightened she really was.

"Let's go," he said, and she gritted her teeth to keep from answering, "Never!"

He helped her onto the back of the huge motorcycle. She fumbled to position her feet, then he slid on in front of her and looked back.

"Comfortable?" he asked with a grin.

Where in God's name should she put her hands? "Snug as a bug," she lied heartily, feeling around furtively. There had to be a hand grip somewhere.

"Here we go."

There was a tremendous roar and the bike lurched forward. Maggie couldn't help it. She screamed.

It wasn't a very loud scream, but David heard it. He brought the machine to a stop again and looked around. "Was that you?" he asked, his eyes dancing with laughter.

"Of course not," she said breathlessly, desperately searching for a place to hold on to, knowing her tightly clenched knees were not going to do the trick. "It must have been the wind."

He laughed. "Come here, you little idiot," he said with rough affection, reaching out to guide her arms around his chest. "This is how you hold on."

She didn't bother to claim she'd known it all along. Her arms clamped around David, holding on for dear life, and they were off.

She couldn't breathe. Her life was flashing before her eyes. The wind whipped at her mouth and she couldn't get any air in. They went around a corner, leaning to the left, and she closed her eyes, sure they were as good as dead.

But no. Soon they were on the straightaway and she began to breathe again. Slowly she gathered the nerve to open her eyes to see where they were going.

They were going so fast! The hard pavement looked so close, and the scenery flew past in such a blur, that her heart was in her throat. But they went a mile or two and nothing terrible happened, so she began to relax.

"I told you you'd love it," David called back.

No, she didn't love it. But she didn't hate it either. And she began to see a bit of what attraction it might hold for a man like David.

And then she began to notice David. She had her arms around his waist. His suit jacket was open and she could feel the hard muscles of his stomach as he leaned into the bike. She could rest her head against his wide shoulders if she wanted to and let his warmth seep into her. It was a very tempting thought, but she fought it.

"Hey," she called when they stopped at a light. "Where are we going?"

Instead of heading into the center of town where the best restaurants were, she saw that they were heading out to the country, passing through farmland already, driving toward the mountains.

"Just wait and see," he called back. "It's dangerous to give you information. You jump to conclusions."

They raced along like the wind, and Maggie began to exult in their flight. It was as though he'd taken her hand and swept her away from the real world into some strange and exotic fantasy only he knew where to find. On and on they rode, and she began to hope they'd never get to their final destination.

CHAPTER THREE

They climbed into the foothills, the mountains purple and imposing before them. Maggie watched the little farms fly past as they sped along the highway, seeing the lemon groves and the walnut orchards in fleeting glimpses. But she realized suddenly that David had taken a side road she'd never been on before.

"Have you ever been down this way?" he asked, turning and smiling at her as they stopped at a railroad crossing.

"No. What is this place?"

He grinned. "I've got a surprise for you." He turned away, gunning the engine and taking off with a roar.

They pulled down off the highway and rode across weeds and rocks down into a stand of trees. Then David killed the engine and Maggie got off, looking around in wonder.

"It's a miniature pine grove out here in the middle of farmland."

He took her helmet off and set it on the seat. "Come on." He folded her hand in his and led her through the trees. "The man who owns this land was from Oregon and he missed the trees, so he tried to bring a bit of his home with him. He planted this. Isn't it wonderful?"

It was. Even the air smelled different. "How did you know about this place?"

"You find a lot of out-of-the-way treasures on a motorcycle." His grin was deliciously seductive. "I found you that way, too."

Maggie was suddenly very uneasy. What was she doing out here in the middle of nowhere with this man? It was time to set ground rules.

"We'd better get going," she said crisply, starting back toward the bike. "You promised me lunch."

"You're right." He took hold of her hand, spinning her back. "I did promise you lunch." His eyes darkened. "Welcome." He pointed out a flat, grassy spot.

She stared at it, then stared at him. "Here?"

He pulled off his suit coat and threw it down on the grassy area. "Here."

She glanced around. There wasn't another soul within miles. "This doesn't look much like a restaurant," she said hesitantly.

"A restaurant?" He snorted. "Who needs a restaurant? Let Mother Nature be our maître d'."

Despite her uneasiness, she almost had to laugh at his comical expression. "What are we going to eat, pine needles?"

He looked pained. "Would I do a thing like that to you?" Reaching into the side bag on his bike, he pulled out a bottle of wine. "You see?" he said, then reached in again and pulled out two candy bars. "I'm ready for anything."

She couldn't help it. She had to laugh. "Do you mean to tell me you always carry around a bottle of wine in your saddlebags?"

"Of course. You never know when you'll meet some lonely lady along the road."

And the next thing she knew she was seated on his suit coat, munching on chocolate-covered peanut butter and sharing sips from a bottle of wine.

"Does Chablis go with peanut butter?" she asked, laughing into his dark eyes.

He considered for a moment, staring at his candy. "It must. I can't really imagine washing this down with a Pinot Noir. Can you?"

"No." The wind stirred the pines and the needles sang. Golden hair blew over her eyes and he reached out, pushing it back, gently touching her cheek. Maggie looked away quickly, her heart pounding.

"Look," he said softly, his face very near to hers. "How close the mountains seem."

She looked up at the snow-covered peaks, trying to ignore the warmth of his breath against her cheek. It was already winter up there, despite the Indian summer weather they were having in the valley. For some reason that made her shiver.

"Have you ever been up there?" he asked softly.

"Just on day trips. I've never backpacked into the wilderness country."

"We ought to go, just you and me. Take a few provisions. Hike to a peak."

She turned slowly to stare at him. "Why?"

His shrug was lazy. "Because it's there," he said carelessly. "Because we want to."

But she didn't want to at all. Looking away, she gazed down into the valley toward Wakefield. She wasn't a horizon chaser, *he* was. He was wild and free, and that scared her.

She popped the last bit of candy bar into her mouth and raised the wine bottle to her lips. "I don't know when I've had a more delicious lunch," she told him.

"I don't know when I've lunched with a more delicious companion," he countered sensuously.

She edged away from him. "We ought to get back."

"Not before dessert," he said.

"What?" Despite all her uneasiness, she was laughing again. "What can you possibly do to top off these awful candy bars?"

"You'll see." He rose and held out a hand to help her up. "Come with me."

There was sensual suggestion in his eyes and she knew she should run—run the other way as fast as she could. But she didn't run. She took his hand and stood beside him, knowing full well he would kiss her if she went with him. The sense of him was so strong—his tall, male body seemed to draw her like a magnet. He held her hand in his and she followed him, powerless to do anything else.

He led her through the trees, into the shadows, and her breath seemed much too short for the easy walk. She wasn't at all sure what he was planning, but she was afraid she was going to wish she'd kept her head later on. But she wouldn't think about that now, not yet.

They heard water and walked toward it. It was only an

irrigation canal, but it had been cut, and rocks strewn about, to make it look like a mountain stream.

"There are streams and trees like this only about half an hour away up in the mountains," Maggie commented. "But this farmer couldn't wait, could he?"

"No." They stood side by side without touching, watching the water. Tiny flowers bloomed about the banks, and lacy ferns nodded in the breeze. The sunlight was dappled as it came through the trees. It was a lovely place.

But Maggie felt nervous as a cat. She'd assumed when he'd brought her here that he was going to make some sort of move. She'd dreaded it, anticipated it, and now that he hadn't done anything, she resented it.

"Nice little view, isn't it?" he murmured, still gazing at the water. "Isn't this just the thing to top off a meal?"

"This is it?" she asked, her voice quavery. "This is dessert?"

He turned toward her, keeping a straight face. "Of course. What did you think I meant?"

She felt a warmth creeping into her cheeks and she turned away. "Nothing," she whispered, but he caught hold of her hand.

"Come on," he insisted, eyes laughing. "What kind of dessert did you have in mind?"

She shrugged, avoiding his eyes.

"Maggie," he said softly. "Be brave. Tell me."

She tossed her head and glared at him in mock defiance. "I thought you were going to throw me in the bushes and make mad passionate love to me. And you know very well that's what you were implying!"

He was laughing and pulling her closer. "Oh, Maggie," he said with a sigh, "don't you know? That's not dessert. That's the bread of life." He gathered her up in his arms, and suddenly his eyes weren't laughing anymore. "We need that just so we won't starve to death," he whispered, and then his lips touched hers and she felt a shiver go through her body, as though something long pent up was being released.

His kiss was warm and tender, and she closed her eyes and let it grow. It felt like him, tasted like him, full of fire and excitement but fully controlled. His beard had just enough growth to be slightly raspy, and as he rubbed his cheek against hers, it seemed to tantalize every nerve ending, sending her pulse skyrocketing, creating an appetite for more and more of him.

His tongue demanded entrance and her lips parted, and then he seemed to be everywhere, devouring her, coaxing her to let go of any control she might still be holding on to.

She was lost, swirling in pure sensation, her mind on hold. She'd never considered herself a passionate woman, but that was only because she'd never felt desire like she was feeling now.

It grew inside her, taking control of her. She was hardly Maggie any longer. She was someone else, someone greedy and demanding. She wanted just as much of him as he wanted of her, and she moaned softly, moving in his embrace, searching for fulfillment.

His hands were at her back, fingers digging in slightly, pressing her to him. She felt her body arch of its own volition. She wanted her breasts hard against him. She wanted to feel him respond. Her fragile control was slipping.

He was pulling her down onto a grassy bed of leaves, and she didn't try to stop him. They lay side by side, and his hand was under her sweater. She could feel the heat of it on her flat stomach and she held her breath, waiting to feel it reach her breast.

She was lost in a misty cloud of desire, and she'd never felt so wonderful before. There'd been groping boys in her past, and men had been lost in the throes of wanting her, but she'd always felt so detached, going through the motions, never really part of the passion. This time it was different. The need for him was burning like a fire within her, its heat spreading, making her reach to feel him closer, closer.

His hand found her breast and she gasped. His fingers teased the nipple and she grabbed him with both hands. His lips left hers and he pushed back the cotton sweater, gazing at the creamy breast with its dusky tip. "Golden girl," he whispered, then looked into her eyes and smiled, touching the hair that flew about her head in a windswept swirl. "My beautiful golden girl."

She stared up at him, suddenly aware of how controlled he still was and of how her control had fled. What had started out as a simple kiss had escalated way beyond that—and *she* was the one who'd urged it on! Stunned at the realization, she lay very still.

Why had he held back? She'd been totally defenseless, and he had carefully, deliberately eased back and given her time to think about what she was doing. Left to her own instincts, she'd have given him everything. But he'd stopped. Why?

"Golden hair," he was murmuring, his warm hand touching her face, "golden skin, golden eyes."

"They're blue," she whispered weakly.

"They look golden with the sun slanting on them this way," he told her softly. "You're my golden girl, Maggie, and I won't hear any argument about it."

She wasn't about to argue with him. She was still too overwhelmed by what she'd just done. She'd offered herself to this man as surely as any gift she'd ever given. He knew it, and yet he'd held back.

As she watched, he leaned down and softly kissed the very tip of her nipple. "A golden girl is a treasure," he said, looking up, and suddenly his eyes were full of some strange emotion she couldn't read. "And treasures aren't usually left lying around." He slowly covered her breast and looked into her eyes. "Do you have a treasure keeper, beautiful Maggie? Someone who thinks you belong to him?"

She swallowed. David Duke fascinated and excited her —and scared her to death. In a moment of unconscious insanity she'd been about to make love with him in the woods. Luckily, that hadn't happened. But now what? Did she dare tempt fate? Something told her she should get away from him as quickly as possible, run away and never look back. Some warning was quivering deep in her soul, telling her to beware. And now he wanted to know if there was someone who thought she belonged to him.

"K-kind of," she whispered.

David's gaze darkened. "Does he want to marry you?" he asked, his voice low and rumbling.

"I . . ." What could she say? Wouldn't it be better if David thought there were someone else? Then she could refuse to see him again, hide from the man who scared her so and have a reasonable excuse. And it wouldn't be a lie, for Bill had mentioned marriage more than once. "Yes."

He grunted, showing he'd known it all along. "Marriage." He said the word as though it were obscene. "I know that's what you want. It's what you're made for. I can see it." He cupped his hand under her chin and forced her to look into his eyes. "But don't do it yet, golden girl. Hold him off. Just give me six months. That's all I ask."

He didn't give her time to answer. His mouth closed on hers, and this time the passion he held leashed within him was so close to the surface, she could feel it pulse. But now she was the one who held back. Her mind was a torrent of swirling doubts, and she didn't dare let her instincts take over again.

He sensed her withdrawal, her confusion, and he pulled away. They lay side by side, both staring at the trees above them. David rose to lean on his elbow, watching her.

"You know what you are, Maggie?" he asked softly. "You're crunchy apples in the fall and daffodils in the spring and football games and Fourth of July picnics. That's what you are."

She squinted, trying to see him clearly with the sunshine coming from behind his head. Though she knew he'd meant his description as a compliment, it stung a bit. "That's what you think," she retorted. "I'm about as much those things as you are Marlon Brando in *The Wild One,* or a desperado, or a heavy metal medley or . . . or a greasy hamburger in a low-down dive."

He chuckled. "Touché. You've got a point there." He reached out and touched her hair. "What's his name?"

She looked up questioningly. "Whose name?"

"The one who wants to marry you."

"Oh." That gave her a qualm, but she'd started this and she'd have to finish it. "Bill Smith."

There was a moment of silence. "You're kidding, aren't you?"

She went up on her elbow to face him. "No, I'm not kidding. Why?"

He laughed. "Oh, come on. You can't be serious. I mean, Maggie Jones and Bill Smith? And you say you aren't ordinary and wholesome as apple pie?"

His hair had been rumpled in their embrace, and she liked the way it fell over his eyes. In fact, despite her misgivings, she liked him, and she was glad they were back to teasing. It was a nice, safe place to be. "They're perfectly good names," she retorted happily. "A lot better than David Duke. What kind of crazy name is that?"

David's chin rose. "It's a name with pride, arrogance, power—not to mention sex appeal."

She raised an eyebrow suspiciously. "You made it up, didn't you?"

He pretended to consider for a moment. "No," he replied at last. "I was born with sex appeal."

She pushed at him with her hand. "No, I mean the name, of course."

"Ah, the name." He looked down at the grass and began shredding a few leaves with his fingers. "The name is my own. It doesn't matter where I got it; it's mine now."

He was still smiling, but something in his voice warned her not to pursue the subject. She lay back down and watched the pine trees blow in the high wind.

"Hear that?" he asked.

"What?" she asked, eyes closed.

"The wind in the pines." She could hear the smile in his voice. "It's got a fine, lonesome sound, doesn't it?"

"Do you really not have any family?" she asked.

He threw down the shards of leaves. "Family?" he said lightly. "What would I need with a family? You only need a family when you're a kid, and I got along fine without one then, too."

"Families are important," she insisted, raising herself on her elbow to gaze at him earnestly. "You must have had a mother and—"

"No." His voice was hard. "Biologically, sure, there had to be a man and woman who got together at some ill-fated moment and created me. But that's as far as it went. I don't owe either of them a damn thing."

Maggie felt cold inside. The anger in him was so real, she could feel it. "But you must have parents—"

He moved like a snake uncoiling, grabbing her wrist and holding it tightly. "I don't want to talk about it, Maggie. Some man and woman conceived me, some woman carried me for nine months, because she couldn't see any way out, and then she got rid of me. It's as simple as that. Subject closed. Okay?"

She nodded, eyes wide, but without thinking she said, "Did you grow up in an orph—" before his hard mouth came down on hers, stopping her words with a kiss so fiery, it took her breath away and wiped all thought from her mind.

And then he was turning away. "It's getting late," he said, getting to his feet and reaching out to help her up. "We'd better get going."

She was shivering, but she followed him back to the motorcycle and climbed on behind him for the long ride home. Her mind was awhirl with questions and doubts. She'd never met a man who brought forth so many contradictory emotions in her.

She slid her arms around him and hung on as the bike roared over a rutted road. That was what a romance with David Duke would be like, she told herself. Holding on for dear life and hoping to survive. She bit her lip and closed her eyes. He wasn't for her, no matter how much she was tempted.

CHAPTER FOUR

"David Duke?" Mark frowned. "Where did you run into that jerk?"

Maggie stared at her brother, surprised by the vehemence of his response. From what she'd seen, most people liked David on sight. Obviously Mark wasn't one of his fans.

The two of them were sitting in their parents' living room, watching the news on television while waiting for dinner. On most nights when Maggie visited she did a lot of the cooking for her mother, but tonight Mildred Jones had something special prepared.

"I met him at the Youth Center," Maggie said, watching her brother lean back in the wide-winged chair, the newspaper on his lap. He was a good-looking man, tall and with a kindly face. But she worried about the perpetual frown between his brows—he was so serious. She wished he'd learn to lighten up a little. If only he would find a girl, someone who suited him. "Why do you call him a jerk?"

"Because he is one." Mark threw down the evening paper and searched his pockets for a cigarette. "I'd call him worse but I wouldn't want to hurt your delicate ears."

That from a man who'd wrestled her for many a stick of gum in his day and called her every name in the book when she won! Maggie grinned. "I think my delicate ears could take it. I know his office is on the same floor as yours. Do you two work together much?"

"Not if I can help it. He's a show-off, and I don't want to have anything to do with him." He found a cigarette and flicked open his lighter. "He walks around the office like God's gift to the electronics industry. He thinks he knows everything. He comes and goes as he pleases, without any consideration for the hours other people work."

Maggie winced, thinking of their long afternoon. Mark took a drag on his cigarette. "And he's got the women in the place acting like they've got a rock star walking the halls." He gave her a halfhearted grin. "As you can see, I'm not too fond of the man."

Maggie turned away and poked at the fire in the fireplace so Mark wouldn't see the color that lit her face when he spoke of the women's reaction to David. She really was a fool, wasn't she? She thought her feelings for David were something special, but of course every woman who saw him wanted to take him home with her. Just a natural reaction to a handsome, charming man. She had to get hold of herself and keep a little perspective.

"He's a consultant?" she asked, trying not to sound too interested.

"Right. The 'genius' they've brought in to solve all our

problems. What he'll do is create a thousand more, then leave us to figure out how to clear them up."

Maggie loved her brother, and even though he was two years older than she was, she'd always felt protective toward him. But right now she couldn't help but think of how dull he must seem to the women at the office when compared to David. She knew without being told that Mark plodded where David soared. Was that why he didn't like David? Did he feel his job was threatened? Or was he right in his assessment that David was really a lightweight in disguise?

"Is it true he's only going to be here for six months?" she asked.

Mark looked at her, mouth open, brow wrinkled. "Oh no, don't tell me you're falling for him too. I can't believe it! I thought you had more sense."

Maggie tried to glare back. "I'm not falling for him! I never said anything of the sort. I'm just—curious about him, that's all."

"I don't understand women," Mark exclaimed, stubbing out his cigarette. "Messing around with a man like that is about as crazy as walking out onto the freeway to play with the cars. It's just plain stupid."

Maggie poked at the fire, watching sparks fly and thinking of David's dark eyes. When you came right down to it, Mark had a very good point.

"What's this in your hair?" Mark leaned forward and pulled a pine needle out of her hair. "Where on earth did you get this?"

Maggie took it from him and turned away to tuck it into her pocket. "I haven't a clue," she lied, gritting her teeth and trying not to blush. She'd been doing more blushing in the last two days than she'd ever done in all the days of her life put together. "Must be from the firewood."

She felt limp as a rag doll. Her day with David had left her torn and confused. It had seemed so easy at first. Her job had been to get him to hire on as a volunteer instructor to start a program teaching the fundamentals of motorcycle riding, care and maintenance to the Winners Club. Either he consented or he didn't. Very black and white. Then something had gone wrong. He'd caught her up in some sort of magic tempest that had led to that crazy scene in the woods.

He'd brought her back to her car in the Farlow Electronics parking lot without saying much more, but she could tell he assumed they'd formed a connection of some sort. For six months. She rolled her eyes in exasperation and paced in front of the fire. Who did he think he was? She wanted to lie down on the floor and kick and scream like a child in a tantrum, he made her so crazy.

She'd done a lot of thinking since he'd left her. Her life had always been orderly, and she wanted it to go on that way. David Duke was a monkey wrench, as far as order went. Despite his professional job and his gorgeous suits, he was just what she'd first suspected—a wild one, a traveler and a taker. He was a drifter with a made-up name. She had to remember what she wanted in life, what was important to her. David Duke didn't fit into that picture.

She spent the rest of the evening trying to wipe him out of her mind. But it was hopeless. Every time she closed her eyes she saw him as he'd looked in the mountains, his hair falling over his forehead in a casual sweep of darkness. He was truly the most exciting man she'd ever met. She decided to stay overnight at her parents', not wanting to risk getting a phone call from him. She couldn't trust herself to turn down anything he might suggest, no matter how outlandish.

By the next evening she felt stronger. She hadn't seen him in over twenty-four hours, and his influence was dimming. So when he called and asked to see her, she turned him down.

"I'm sorry, David. I'm busy tonight."

"How about tomorrow night?"

"I'm working at the Youth Center. It's my night to chaperon the junior high dance."

There was a moment of silence, during which the only thing she heard was the loud beating of her own heart. "And what is it that you're busy doing tonight?" he asked at last, his voice emotionless.

"David, that's really not—"

"Any of my business?" He was quiet again, and when he finally spoke his voice was hard. "It's the fellow who wants you to marry him, isn't it?"

She hesitated. Bill *was* coming over, but agreeing would just perpetuate the lie she'd set in David's mind. She wasn't marrying Bill, not ever.

But David mistook her silence for acknowledgment and said, "Well, that's your choice, I guess." There was a strange cheerfulness to his tone. "But I don't know what I'm going to do with myself tonight. Kitty's busy, too."

It took a moment for Maggie to remember that Kitty

was the orangutan she'd recommended he date. Despite the tension of their exchange, she found herself smiling.

"I'm sure you've got better resources than that," she said. "From what I've heard, half the women at Farlow are swooning over you."

"It could be half the women in the state, and it still wouldn't be worth one kiss from you, golden girl," he said. The words were sweet, but the tone of his voice was harsh. "So you've decided to walk on the safe side of the street, have you? It could get boring, Maggie. But I wish you luck." And then there was nothing but a click on the other end of the line.

"That's it," she whispered to herself, staring at the receiver. "The end. He won't call again."

She was shaking when she hung up, and then, suddenly, there were tears in her eyes for no apparent reason. She went into the bathroom and turned on the shower as hard and hot as she could stand, stripped and stood under the water until she had cried herself out.

Bill came over for coffee and a talk after dinner. It was the sort of get-together they often had. He'd offered to take her to a movie that evening, but she refused, knowing she wouldn't be able to keep her mind on the story. "Let's just talk," she'd suggested.

"All right." Bill was tall and spare and looked more like a working farmer than the heir to a farming fortune. "But I can think of things I'd rather do."

"Oh?" she murmured absently, stirring her coffee with her spoon. "Like what?"

"Oh, I don't know." He coughed discreetly. "Like trying to revive our love affair, maybe."

"What?" She glanced up, surprised. "What love affair?"

He looked pained. "You don't even remember?"

She laughed gently and reached out to take his hand. "Oh, you mean that nice friendly dating relationship we've had all these months? Bill, I—I never think of it as a love affair."

He rolled his eyes. "Obviously not. I don't suppose you'd want to let the thought linger in your mind for a while? Sort of see if it takes hold?" His smile was sad. "After all, we like each other pretty well. Maybe that would be as good as love in the long run."

A week before she might have been at least partially persuaded by his arguments, but no more. She'd never really been in love, but she'd met David Duke, and she knew what she felt for him so far surpassed her mild affection for Bill as to put it in another solar system.

David's dark face appeared in her thoughts and she sighed. She could only trust that what she felt for him was a passing thing, like a fever, and she'd get over it soon.

But to her dismay, it hung on. And the funny thing was, she missed him. Missed him! A man she hardly knew. He hadn't even existed for her a week before. How could he possibly have changed her life so much that she missed him?

But she did. Whenever someone came in through the door of the Youth Center, she looked up quickly, hoping it would be him. While she ate her lunch at the corner hamburger stand, she found herself scanning the passing crowd, looking for a tall man with black hair. And alone at home in her apartment, he seemed to be hiding in every shadow.

"You're nuts," Cathy told her bluntly. "He's adorable. Go out with him. Enjoy him while you have the chance."

"Like a movie or a carnival that's passing through town?" Maggie answered scathingly. "No thanks. He's not my type."

"Why not?" Cathy probed. "I mean, after all, you don't have to marry the guy. I doubt if you could, even if you wanted to. He doesn't really seem like the marrying type, does he? So just have some fun."

Maggie glared at her friend. "If you like him so much, why don't *you* go out with him?"

Cathy grinned like a Cheshire cat. "No way. We're too much alike. We'd be like two comets colliding in the night sky." She leaned back and sighed dreamily. "I need a quiet man, a steady man . . ." Looking at Maggie out of the corner of her eye, she asked, "How's Mark these days?"

"Hmm?" Maggie scarcely heard her, her mind was so filled with not thinking about David. "Same as always." Then she remembered something. "Oh, you know, I've been meaning to tell you. You'll be pleased to hear that Mark's found a girlfriend."

If Maggie had been paying more attention she might have noticed the stricken look on Cathy's face. "Who?" she asked, her green eyes wide.

"Sheila Carter. She's a secretary at Farlow, real cute

and quiet, just Mark's style." She shrugged. "Who knows? Maybe he'll finally fall in love."

"Whoopee," said Cathy sarcastically.

But Maggie had turned away, still thinking about David. The man was taking over her life! She had to find a way to forget all about him.

She saw him in town once, riding down Main Street on his red motorcycle. She was coming out of the post office and there he was, heading for the mountains. He didn't see her, but her heart leapt at the sight of him and her legs were weak for the next hour. It was so ridiculous—she was acting like a silly teenager. Surely she would get over him soon!

The week dragged by. On Saturday morning Maggie woke with a start, remembering she'd invited two girlfriends from her high school days to breakfast. About once a month she and her old friends spent the morning playing tennis; each took turns providing breakfast after the game. Today it was Maggie's turn. She'd forgotten all about it, and there wasn't a thing to eat in the house. Groaning, she pulled herself out of bed, threw on an old sweatshirt and a faded pair of jeans, and made her way to the mom-and-pop grocery on the corner, the only store nearby that was open at that time on a Saturday morning.

The little market was full of people, but luckily Maggie didn't see anyone she knew. Still half-asleep, she picked up a quart of milk and a carton of eggs and turned toward the bakery shelf. There was one package of sweet rolls left, but there was a knot of people standing in front of the display. She edged toward the rolls, saying "Excuse me" and reaching around a large woman who was directly in her way. But just as her fingers touched the crinkly cellophane of the package, it was snatched away in the other direction.

"Oh no," she moaned, turning to see who'd stolen her rolls. As the crowd cleared out, she found herself staring up into David's dark eyes. He was holding the package of sweet rolls, gazing at her speculatively.

For just a second she wondered if she was seeing things. She blinked, focusing her eyes, but he didn't disappear. There he was, large as life, wearing gray slacks and a black turtleneck sweater under his leather jacket. She suddenly remembered what she looked like and wished the floor would open and swallow her up.

"You look about fourteen," David said at last.

"You look as though you haven't been to bed yet," she retorted. And he did. His eyes were heavy-lidded and slightly bloodshot, his hair was mussed. And he looked tired.

"You're right," he replied shortly. "Not my own, anyway."

She stiffened, wounded even though she had no right to be. Then he swore softly to himself, realizing that what he'd said had been meant to hurt her. "I've been working," he admitted gruffly. "We had a major debugging job to do."

She shook her head, avoiding his eyes. It was none of her business what he did with his nights. He'd offered her a place in his life—even if temporarily—and she'd refused it. It wasn't his fault if she couldn't get him out of her mind. She wanted to close her eyes and pretend he wasn't there.

But he *was* there. And she knew by the way she was trembling that he could sweep her up and carry her away with him if he wanted to. Why was she so weak around him? Did he know how badly she wanted to drop everything and run into his arms? If he did, he gave no sign. He just stood before her, holding the breakfast rolls.

"Want to arm-wrestle for them?" he asked softly, but there was no humor in his eyes. Instead he seemed to be waiting, watching for something.

"You got them first," she said, starting to back away. "I'll just have to make do with eggs and a loaf of bread."

He held them higher and looked at the package. "We might be able to figure out some sort of compromise," he suggested dryly. "We could divide them." He glanced at her, his eyes hooded. "Or we could eat them all at my place."

"Oh, but I've got someone . . ." Her voice trailed off. She was thinking fast, wondering if she could possibly stand up her friends, and while she wasn't paying attention, David was misinterpreting what she'd said.

"I see," he said coldly, and when she looked up again, his eyes were dark and hard as glass, with something flickering behind the barrier, something open and aching. "Good old Bill, I suppose. Waiting back at your place for breakfast, is he?" He threw the sweet rolls into her arms and she very nearly dropped the rest of her parcels. "Take them," he said gruffly. "I'm not hungry anymore."

She watched numbly as he strode from the building, and then she heard his motorcycle roar off onto the highway. Maybe it was for the best, she told herself. But it didn't feel like it.

The hurt, vulnerable look that had been in his eyes haunted her all day. Was he really upset that she might prefer another man? Had his male pride been hurt, or was he really jealous about her?

The whole thing was ludicrous, she told herself. He didn't care about her. He was the original model for devil-may-care! Every girl in town was crazy for him, so why would he let a little thing like a rejection from Maggie Jones bother him? And yet she couldn't shake the feeling that she'd hurt him, and she ached to do something to take away the pain.

She couldn't even escape him at night. She had trouble falling asleep, and when she finally dropped off, she found David lurking in her dreams.

He was riding the black motorcycle but without the helmet, and he threw his head back and laughed as he rode. She was upstairs in a two-story house. It seemed to be her parents' house, and she seemed to be in her old bedroom, looking out the window. David rode around and around the house, never looking up to see her, and she hung out the window like Rapunzel, somehow not knowing how to get down to where David was, as though stairways didn't exist. She wanted to get to him so badly, and finally she leapt out, hoping to jump down to where he was. But something went wrong and instead of landing on the ground, suddenly she was flying off into the clouds, leaving David far behind.

When she woke up she felt as though her whole body were clenched like a fist. It took a half-hour of yoga exercises and a long hot bath before she could relax enough to go to sleep again, and by that time the Sunday sky was turning peach-colored and she was due to help Burt for the day.

CHAPTER FIVE

The three donated dirt bikes had been delivered to the Youth Center on Saturday afternoon, and on Sunday most of the Winners showed up to try them out. None of the boys knew much about riding and the results were pathetic, including a sprained ankle and two bent fenders. Burt was in despair.

"I don't know what we're going to do, Maggie," he wailed. "I've questioned the men who come into the gym, trying to find one who rides and can give us a hand, but as soon as they find out I want them for the Winners, they back off. No one wants to work with these kids. I couldn't even get the guy who donated the bikes to stick around and help."

"They're bright kids," Maggie said soothingly. "They'll figure it out for themselves."

"Sure, there are a few of them who will—the real winners. But there are kids in that group who won't, kids who need that extra help an adult could give them. The ones who'll fall through the cracks if someone doesn't hold them back. And those are the ones who need this most." He looked at her, his hazel eyes wide and suffering. "I don't suppose you could try David Duke again?"

Maggie watched him and shook her head. "Oh, Burt . . ."

He waved a hand at her. "Never mind. I'm sorry I asked. We'll muddle through, somehow."

The boys were taking turns in the middle of the track when Maggie and her girls arrived Monday afternoon, but while she and the gymnasts jogged and did calisthenics, the boys seemed more interested in whistling and making comments to the girls as they passed.

"They're watching us!" the girls wailed, but Maggie made them go through their routine anyway, hoping the boys would tire of the view and get back to learning to ride. There was no adult with them, which was a problem. What was Burt thinking of, letting them loose with the bikes on their own? The boys were going to run wild if there was no one to corral them.

One boy in particular, who seemed to be the best at riding, nosed his motorcycle in front of Randi as she was passing, stopping her in her tracks.

"Hey," he said, his blue eyes narrowed with pretended disdain. "You got freckles like that anywhere else besides your face?" His gaze flicked arrogantly over her young body. He was a handsome kid with chestnut brown hair and cobalt blue eyes. Maggie had noticed Randi eyeing him earlier, but he didn't seem to have a smooth way of getting to know girls who attracted him.

However, Randi was not to be cowed. "That's something you'll never know," she said coyly, maneuvering around the bike. "You can spend the rest of your life trying to figure it out."

Maggie let the first incident pass, but when he stopped

Randi again and they struck up a longer conversation, she decided it was time to put a stop to it. Looking at the two of them, she could see that leaving them together was like rubbing two sticks on a dry, windy day—something was bound to catch on fire.

She lined up her girls for the march down to the gym, then left them at the top of the stairs. "All right, Winners, I want you all here in the middle of the field," she called, waiting while they straggled over. "I believe you were all sent up here to work with the motorcycles, not to interrupt the gymnastics warm-up," she said, gazing into one pair of hostile eyes after another. "Next time I want you to leave the girls alone."

"What's the matter?" the boy who'd stopped Randi asked sarcastically. "Can't the little rich girls take it? You gotta protect them from us *bad boys?*"

She stared at him. "What's your name?" she asked softly.

"Jed Marker," he admitted after a moment's hesitation.

"These are not rich girls, Jed. They're from families very much like yours." She had to admit that was stretching a point. Most of the girls were from modest families, though one, Randi Farlow, happened to be from a wealthy background. "Please give them the same respect you'd expect them to give you."

She knew her little speech wasn't a real grabber and probably wouldn't do much good, but she wasn't sure what else she could say.

She could hardly keep her mind on training that afternoon. She put the girls through a tumbling routine and stared into space, feeling almost as though she were losing her mind. It was very simple really, she kept telling herself. On the one hand, she could go on as before, pretending David didn't exist and being miserable. Or she could give in to temptation and go to David again. Then she might be able to get him to come and help with the motorcycles, making Burt and the boys happy. But she would surely find herself falling under David's spell again, and be miserable when he left.

That was the choice. Misery now, or misery later.

When it was finally time for the girls to go home, Maggie hurried them out the door and went to find Burt, who was organizing the boys in a basketball game.

"Who is your very worst rider?" she asked.

"What?" Burt's friendly face was creased with confusion.

"The clumsiest guy. The one who always crashes."

"Jimmy White. He can't even shift gears."

"Good. Have the boys pack one of the motorcycles into a trailer and let me take Jimmy with me."

Burt shook his head in bewilderment. "Where are you going?"

"On a wild goose chase," she told him. "But it's worth a try."

It occurred to her as she left the Youth Center that she might be working herself up for nothing. For all she knew, David might have lost all interest in her by now, and it would serve her right. But she suppressed the thought. If that was true, a whole new level of misery awaited her and there was no use thinking about it.

The parking lot at Farlow Electronics was half-empty

when they arrived. Most of the office staff would have left at five, but Maggie knew from experience that the programmers would still be there. That was one drawback to this scheme—the programmers might stay until midnight, for all she knew. All she could do was hope that they wouldn't work too late tonight.

She pulled the truck up beside David's motorcycle and ran back to help Jimmy unload the dirt bike. "You stay right here," she told him, "and wait for my signal. Then you start the engine and try to ride up and down the parking lot."

Jimmy was a small boy, skinny and wary-looking. He wasn't sure what this was all about, but he was game and ready to do as Maggie ordered. He stayed on the bike, which looked two sizes too big for him, while Maggie ran to the front of the building, where she could see the elevators opening and disgorging workers. Ten long minutes dragged by before she saw anyone she knew.

"Hi, Maggie," Cassie said, walking out with a spring in her step. "You looking for David Duke again?"

Maggie hesitated. She didn't want him to know she was here until he came out. "Sort of," she admitted. "Do you know what he's doing?"

Cassie pretended to swoon. "No, but I wish I did. What a hunk!" She looked at Maggie and shook her head. "You're going to have to get in line, girl. Every woman in there between eighteen and fifty is gunning for him."

Maggie joined in her laughter but it was an effort—she really didn't see the humor in the situation herself. She watched Cassie walk to her car, then looked back at the lobby. Time stretched excruciatingly. Fifteen minutes. Twenty minutes.

"Maggie," Jimmy called. "How much longer do you think?"

The poor kid. She hated to leave him standing there, holding the bike up and wishing he were anywhere else. But this was for a good cause.

And then she saw David coming. "Now!" she called to Jimmy and was delighted to hear the motorbike engine roar into action. She looked around quickly to make sure there was no one backing out of a parking space and no one walking past whom Jimmy might damage. Then she made her way back to the truck. "Just take it easy," she told Jimmy, craning to see David coming out the entrance. "Up and down the parking lot."

The young boy made a valiant attempt, but the bike stalled as he tried to change gears. He got it going again, and then ran into a planting bunker before he got up any speed. The bike almost fell over. By that time David had reached Maggie's side.

"Don't tell me; let me guess," he said, dark eyes shining. "This has got to be one of the kids from the Youth Center."

She nodded, not meeting his gaze. "I thought I'd bring him over here to get a little practice in the parking lot," she said easily. "I'm sure the Farlows won't mind."

David was quiet for a moment while they watched Jimmy stall again. "Well, he does need the practice," David admitted dryly.

"Try kicking it harder, Jimmy," Maggie called helpfully.

"No," David called to counter her suggestion. "Lean back a little so your weight is over the starter."

Jimmy did as David instructed, and the engine came to life again. David looked at Maggie and started to laugh. "I know what you're trying to do, golden girl," he said softly. "What makes you think such an obvious ploy will work on me?"

She looked up into his dark eyes and realized she'd been starving for the sight of him. "If this doesn't work, I'll try something else," she said, steeling herself against his charm.

"I'd like to see what you'd come up with," he murmured thoughtfully. "In fact, maybe I could give you a few ideas of things that just might work."

He touched her gently on her shoulder, and she shivered, pulling away. Jimmy's motorcycle fell over at that moment, and they both ran to him. David pulled the bike up and helped Jimmy to his feet. He gave him some advice on how to sit and how to move, and sent him on his way again.

"Are they all this bad?" he asked at last, watching the boy.

"Just about."

He sighed and turned to her. "Listen, maybe I could just come over a few times . . ."

A grin began to spread over her pretty face, a grin that started in the soles of her feet and was warming everything between there and her face. "Really?"

He cursed softly and turned her to face him with two hands on her shoulders. "Yeah, really," he said, disgusted with himself. Then his eyes darkened, and she caught a hint of a deeper emotion. "But I'm not a volunteer, Maggie," he said slowly. "I expect to be paid. And I don't come cheap."

"Oh—oh dear," she stammered. "I'm afraid we don't have the funds—"

"Funds, hell," he said roughly. His dark eyes searched hers, and he seemed to see something there that reassured him. Slowly he grinned. "I want you. And I'll take the first payment right now. Kiss me."

The arrogance of the man!

"David!" she gasped, looking around to see if anyone had heard. "No!"

"Wrong answer, golden girl," he said, pulling her to him.

She thrust up her hands to ward him off, but they slid beneath his suit coat and landed against his chest. It was so warm there, so intoxicatingly seductive. . . .

"David, don't!" she insisted, but he did, smothering her protests with his hot, dizzying kiss.

The kiss went on and on. Maggie stopped struggling very soon, her fingers spread against his chest, reveling in the heat. And then she found that she didn't want him to stop. She was dimly aware of other people passing, but she didn't care. He was kissing her in front of everyone. Did that mean that what he'd said was true, that he wanted her more than he wanted any other woman around? She clung to his lips and hated herself—but she couldn't stop.

Someone else was coming near, someone who wasn't passing. Someone who was going to break the spell and bring her back to reality. She sighed, knowing it was inevitable.

"Maggie?" Mark's voice was rough with outrage. "Is that really you?"

Maggie felt David pulling away from her, and she wanted to reach out and draw him back. "Go away, Mark," she murmured drowsily.

David stiffened, turning to Mark. "Is this another one?" he asked, and Maggie realized he meant another Bill Smith, another rival. His voice was hard, and when she looked into his face, she realized with a start that David could be terribly tough if he wanted to be.

"No," she said quickly. "Mark is my brother."

David relaxed immediately. "No kidding." He grinned. "I should have known. Both Joneses. And both giving me so much trouble."

"I don't know what you think you're doing here, Maggie," Mark said, ignoring David. "But you're making a scene in front of the whole company."

"Street theater," David told him authoritatively. "Haven't you heard of it? You set up shop in a common, busy place and dramatize—"

Mark didn't think he was funny. "I don't think you should be kissing my sister here," he snapped, eyes blazing.

David's smile was wicked. "You're right. I should take her somewhere private where I could kiss her properly. Good advice, Jones. How about my apartment, Maggie?"

Maggie knew he was goading her brother but she laughed anyway. She looked at him and felt warm and wonderful, and she knew she'd been missing this feeling since the last time they were together. She needed him, she wanted him. She had to face it, and there was no turning back. She'd go to his apartment. She'd go with him to the moon.

"She can't come with you," Mark said with smug satisfaction. "She's due at our parents' for dinner." He eyed Maggie questioningly.

"Oh, dear! I'd forgotten all about it. What time is it?" She glanced at her watch, then looked up into David's face. How could she leave him here now that she'd acknowledged her need for him? "Would you—would you like to come too?" she offered hopefully.

"Thanks, but I don't think so."

She looked at Mark for support, but feeling his job was done, he grimaced at her and walked away to his parked car.

"My parents would love to have you," she said, wishing she knew why he looked so distant all of a sudden. "Really, when I lived with them, I was always bringing home . . ."

"Strays you found in the street?" His voice was hard, his voice cold. "No thanks. I'm not into family get-togethers, Maggie. I didn't have much practice at that sort of thing when I was growing up."

"Oh, but you'd have a good time, I'm sure . . ."

David ran his fingers through her hair, holding her head in a grasp that was as much a warning as a caress. "No family affairs," he said bluntly. "I don't like them." His dark eyes searched hers. "I want to be with you, but you've got to understand: I'm not like your Bill Smith who wants to build a life. I'm traveling through. If you want to spend some time with me, I'd like that. But don't try to take me home to mother."

She nodded quickly, but she didn't really understand. "But tomorrow night I've got pool duty . . ."

His face was still cold, impassive, almost frightening in the way he seemed to be able to block out emotion. "Good things are worth waiting for," he told her, but he wasn't smiling. "I'll wait for you, Maggie. At least for a while."

What had she done, promising him things? He confused her, scared her. What on earth was she letting herself in for?

But even as the fears formed in her mind, he leaned down and kissed her once again, softly, tenderly, and she clung to him as though she could never get enough. Then he raised his head and gestured toward Jimmy, who was still gamely riding about the parking lot. "Get your bait back to the Youth Center. I'll see you there tomorrow." His rakish grin was the last thing she saw before he pulled the helmet over his head and kicked his motorcycle into action.

CHAPTER SIX

David took a length of paper as long as a football field, all covered with computer listings, and squashed it down, trying to stuff it into his small wastepaper basket. Realizing that it would never fit, he let it trail out like the tail of a huge paper dragon, fluttering across the floor of his office, while his gaze flickered to his silver watch.

In just half an hour he planned to run over to the Youth Center. Maggie would be there. So would the boys he'd promised to teach all the fine points of riding to. But it was the picture of Maggie's sweet face that filled his mind, pleasing and disturbing at the same time.

David liked women. He liked the way they moved, the way their hair swayed when they walked, the way they looked up at him with eyes full of hope and wonder, trying to anticipate where he was headed. Soft skin; silky hair; a full, rounded breast just begging to fill a masculine hand; wide hips just waiting to cradle his—women were part of the joy and beauty of life. He couldn't imagine happiness without them.

But he never really thought about them much. Handsome and charming as he was, he'd never had to go out looking for them. They came to him, usually in numbers larger than he could handle. They were available, like food and water and shelter for the night. In any new area he moved into, it was usually more difficult to find a good riding area than it was to find entertaining and accommodating women.

For some reason, though, he hadn't messed around much here in Wakefield. The usual women had traipsed in and out, smiling the usual come-ons, making the usual suggestive jokes, flirting with their eyes, their touches. And he hadn't been tempted to follow up once. Only one woman in the entire town had caught his interest, and she'd done more running away than anything else.

There was a theory, he knew, that men who were addicted to the chase went after women who ran away. He'd never subscribed to that theory himself. He didn't need the thrill of the chase—he got enough thrills with his riding. Under normal circumstances, when Maggie had first resisted his charm, he would have shrugged and turned away, forgetting her in a moment as the next beauty came into view. But there was something about sweet, hometown Maggie. . . .

He wanted her. Deep down inside there was a fire burning, a hot, fierce desire for her, that was nothing like he'd ever felt before. And just the fact that it was so different, so much stronger than anything he was used to, made him hesitate to go out and get her. He could have her, he knew it. He could have had her that day in the pines. So why the hell hadn't he done it already and gotten her out of his system?

He frowned, feeling unsure and not liking it.

With an oath he rose from his desk, paced to the window, then out into the hall. Maggie's brother's office was just a few steps away. He and Mark weren't friendly, but he found himself drawn in through Mark's open door. Mark was at his work station, staring at the screen.

"Hey, Mark, how's it going?" David said with false geniality. He glanced at the work displayed on the screen. "Aren't you going to initialize that stuff?"

Mark looked up, his blue eyes hooded. He typed in his initials, then saved his work, turned off the computer and turned in his swivel chair to face David. Keeping his eyes on the other man, Mark pulled open a drawer and drew a large, flat object out.

"I've got something to show you," he said with his usual deliberate delivery. He set a large wooden picture frame out on his desk, right in front of David. "I'm having this made up as a surprise for Maggie. What do you think?"

David looked down without much interest at first, but his eye was caught by that same face that had been haunting him all day and he looked more closely. What he saw was a collage of childhood pictures, beautifully done so that they all made a whole, a panoply of Maggie's growing years: Maggie on a tricycle, small face frowning in concentration; Maggie learning to ride a two-wheeler, Mark holding on to the bike, guiding her along; Maggie throwing a baton into the air, her coltish legs sticking out beneath a short red-and-silver skirt, her face beaming with pride; Maggie with a gap-toothed grin; Maggie dressed for the senior prom, her eyes full of stars.

David stared at the pictures. He couldn't take his eyes

off them. He knew he should chuckle; he should grin and say, "Boy, she's really grown up, hasn't she?" He should laugh the whole thing off, forget it. But he couldn't. The pictures did just what Mark had hoped they would do—put Maggie in a whole new perspective. David's heart felt like a piece of lead in his chest.

"Nice," he muttered, frowning slightly. "I'm sure she'll like it."

He looked into Mark's face and for the first time that he could remember, he had the urge to avoid another man's eyes. Steeling himself, he smiled instead. "You two get along pretty well for siblings, don't you?"

Mark didn't answer directly. His light eyes were intense. "She's not the local virgin, you know," he said softly, holding David's gaze with fierce determination. "Like your friend was telling you to find. She's not some notch to put on your scorecard. She's a real person, with a life, a soul, a heart. Don't break it."

David straightened, pulling away, but his usual sense of humor had completely deserted him and he couldn't think of a thing to say.

"We love her," Mark went on, his voice toneless but all the more effective for that. "We don't want to see her hurt."

"I wouldn't hurt your sister for anything in the world," David said, his voice harsh. "I don't go around hurting people for the fun of it, Mark."

Mark's eyes narrowed. "Are you going to tell me you've never hurt a woman before?" he asked accusingly. "Are you going to tell me they all know exactly what they're getting with you? That they all take things as lightly as you do? That they always forget you as quickly as you forget them? Are you going to tell me you've never led someone on and then deserted her?"

David stepped forward, leaning aggressively toward Mark. His dark eyes smoldered with outrage. "This is the eighties, Jones," he said evenly. "Women aren't victims any longer, or hadn't you heard? They're equal partners these days." He glanced down at the picture, then away again. "Maggie knows the score. She's an adult. She can make her own choices." His finger came down on the picture of Maggie on the bicycle. "She doesn't need her big brother to hold her up anymore. Let go, Mark. Or you just may find yourself lying in the dust with tire tracks on your back."

Mark didn't say any more, and even if he had, David wouldn't have heard him. He slammed out of the office and out of the building and was still steaming when he arrived on his motorcycle in the parking lot at the Youth Center.

Maggie had never felt so alive. Her body seemed to tingle with anticipation. She heard the motorcycle outside and her heart gave a small lurch. He was here.

"Okay, guys," she said, turning to the group of youngsters sitting with her in the lobby. "Mr. Duke is here."

Jed Marker twitched his rangy shoulders and looked at her sullenly from beneath lowered brows. He was wearing faded jeans with holes at the knees and a shapeless T-shirt that said *Super Stud* across his chest. "Do we have to call him mister?" he asked with just the suggestion of a sneer.

Maggie hesitated. She was so eager for everything to go right. "It would be nice. At least until you get to know him better. And then he might suggest you call him David." She could see the resistance in Jed's callowly handsome face. "After all, Jed, he's an expert in his field and someone to respect. Calling him mister is just an acknowledgment of how we feel about him."

"Hell, let's just call him Your Majesty and forget it," the teenager muttered.

The others tittered, but before Maggie had a chance to admonish Jed, David's long shadow fell through the doorway, and then he was there himself, filling the room with his dark, compelling presence.

Maggie jumped up. Her eyes met his across the room and she shivered, then flushed, hoping he hadn't noticed. Her chin rose. She was determined to remain cool and collected. "Mr. Duke," she said quickly. "We're so glad you could make it."

David's smile swept across her; then his eyes turned to the boys in the room. They moved restlessly under his gaze, but even Jed didn't seem prepared to say anything challenging just yet. He watched David closely, his face closed, his eyes guarded.

David took his time. Maggie had been a little worried about what kind of teacher he would be, but her doubts fell away quickly. The man had all the confidence in the world. He knew better than to display any chink in his armor before this audience. "So you fellows think you want to learn about riding, do you?" he said quietly, examining each face in turn.

The boys looked at one another and nodded, but no

one spoke. There was an air of waiting, of uncertainty. These boys who'd been so enthusiastic about this program just hours before were suddenly acting as though they couldn't care less.

Maggie felt a moment's panic. What if David was turned off by this attitude? What if he used it as an excuse to back out? She started to step forward, ready to bridge the gap she could sense forming, but a raised eyebrow from David held her in check. He didn't need her help. She'd asked him to come do this, and he would do it his way. Reading all that in his glance in an instant, Maggie stepped back, leaving it to him.

David looked from one boy to another slowly, searchingly. "Hey, guys, I'm ready to teach you everything I know about motorcycles. But I'm not into force-feeding. You've got to want it."

The boys looked from David to Jed, ready to take their cue from their natural leader. Jed's face was blank of any expression. He stared back at David. Maggie could see that his reaction would chart the course for them all. She waited, holding her breath.

"What's with the suit?" Jed asked at last, his voice and expression full of disdain. "You gonna wear that on the bike?"

David looked down at his suit, and Maggie could see him smothering a grin. "What's wrong with my suit?" he asked innocently.

Jed shifted weight from one leg to the other and hooked his thumbs in the belt of his jeans. "Bike riders don't wear suits," he said, his lip curling with disgust.

"They do if they want to make a living where I work,"

David responded evenly. "They do if they want to be taken seriously in the business world." He studied the unconvinced expression on Jed's face for a long moment, then smiled. "But I usually don't wear a suit when I'm going to do some heavy riding, you're right there. I've got some other clothes to change into here in my bag. I'll be putting them on in just a few minutes." Dropping the bag, he began to pull at the knot in his tie. "What's your name?" he asked Jed.

Jed's chin rose defiantly. "Jed Marker."

"What have you got against suits, Jed Marker?" David asked, pulling the tie out and draping it across a nearby chair.

Jed shrugged. "I don't have anything against suits. Just the people who wear them."

David shrugged out of his suit coat and slung it across the chair, beginning to work on the buttons of his shirt. "Taking things at face value seems to be an ingrained habit in this town," he murmured, glancing at Maggie. The starched white shirt was off and David stood before them in a sleeveless undershirt, his brown, muscular shoulders gleaming in the afternoon sunshine that slanted in through the plate glass windows. The effect was stunning. In a handful of seconds he'd gone from the elegant grace of a men's fashion plate to the earthy sensuality of a primal masculine animal.

Maggie had to look away. She could hardly breathe, hardly believe what she was going through. She'd never in all her life had such a response to a man. It was like a current that swept her off her feet, a wild wind that sprang up out of nowhere and took her breath away.

David Duke was a force of nature, something akin to the pulse of life, something she'd never known about before —but something that made her feel so alive, so excited, she couldn't imagine letting it slip away.

Still, she didn't want anyone to know. Glancing around quickly, she was relieved to see that the others were paying no attention to her and her reactions. Even David was watching the boys and hadn't noticed.

"How's this?" he was asking Jed. "Better? Do I pass as a cycle rider now?"

The boys snickered and shuffled their feet. Jed glanced at Maggie's strained face, and a reluctant grin grew along the edges of his mouth. He shrugged, digging his hands deep into frayed pockets. "Yeah," he muttered. "I guess so."

"Good." David collected his clothes, picked up his bag and gestured toward the upper field. "Get on up there and wait for me. We're going to get right to work. I entered you all in the county championships six weeks away, and you don't want to look like a bunch of fools in front of the whole county, do you?"

"What?" Maggie was appalled, quickly forgetting her embarrassment. Maybe she hadn't impressed upon him just how bad at riding these kids were. "But they don't know the first thing about how to ride!"

David shrugged. "They will by then." He looked at their stunned faces. "Go on up and wait for me. Unless you've got something better to do."

The boys didn't seem quite sure what to make of David yet, but they weren't ready to push it. Shuffling their feet and casting surreptitious glances at David as they passed, they filed out of the lobby and up toward the field. Once they'd left, David swung around and smiled at Maggie.

"How'd I do, boss?" he asked, eyes sparkling.

She wanted to laugh, just for sheer joy, just for being so close to him, within range of his deep, seductive voice. Maybe, she thought a bit wildly, she would laugh and he would laugh and he would pull her into his arms and they would somehow become joined, fused so tightly that no one would ever be able to tell where one began and the other ended. The temptation was great, and she almost gave in. But something—some shadow, some trick of light in his eyes—stopped her, left her just unsure enough to hesitate. She looked away and swallowed hard.

"I . . . just fine." She smiled and looked back again. Yes, he had done fine, though she'd had a few rough moments of uncertainty. Then her smile faded as anxiety returned. "But what is all this about county championships? They'll never be ready for that!"

He shrugged, drawing her gaze back to his magnificent shoulders, making her flush again. "You don't have goals, you never get anywhere." He said it with such finality, she knew it was part of the creed he lived by. "I'm not doing this just for the fun of it, you know."

"I know that." She smiled. "More like under duress, I'd say."

"No." He closed the distance between them with one quick step, and suddenly his hand was in her hair, his fingers tangling in the curls, and he was so close, she felt the heat of his body flood over her. Her hands touched the naked strength of his arms, stroking him with a hunger she hadn't known she could possess.

He looked down at her hands on his tan skin and felt a sudden surge of power. She was his for the taking. She was helpless in a way no woman had ever been with him before. He could mold her, form her, and all he had to do was speak. Somehow that made him more gentle. He had to be careful with this woman.

"Duress had nothing to do with it," he murmured, his face near hers. "I've got a goal here, just like I always do. I'm working for high wages this time, Maggie Jones." Could she feel the fire in him as he could feel it in her? Was she experienced enough to know just how good they were going to be together?

His hands drew her closer as his lips grazed her temple, and he whispered, "I want you. Tonight."

Her breath was coming fast, her eyelids drifting closed. In another moment she would surrender right here in the lobby. "All right," she whispered back, not letting herself think about what she was promising.

"Good." His lips touched hers briefly, warm and firm and hinting at what was to come. "I'd better get changed."

His hand slid out of her hair and then he was moving away. Her knees nearly buckled beneath her, and she reached out for a chair to keep from falling.

"Tonight," he said again, his smile just for her. He turned and walked toward the locker rooms.

She watched until he was out of sight, then turned away from the doorway with a smile she couldn't hold back. She stopped short when she found Burt watching her, standing in the entry to his office. There was a puzzled look in his kindly eyes, a worried wrinkle across his forehead, and for just a moment she was horrified, wondering what he'd heard.

"Maggie?" he asked. "Maggie, do you think . . . ?"

Not really aware of what he was about to say, Maggie knew instinctively she didn't want to hear it. What could he say, after all, that she hadn't already said to herself? She knew David was a drifter, a playboy and all those other words for a type that was guaranteed to break her heart. Burt wanted to warn her, but it was too late for that.

"No time to think, Burt," she said as she breezed past him toward her own office. Happiness was still running wild inside her and she didn't want to risk stemming the flow. "I've got to call the health department about those pool inspections."

He watched her go, but the worried look didn't leave his face. "Damn," he whispered to himself. "I never thought she might fall for him. What have I done?"

A little over an hour later David sat in Burt's office, filling out an information form about his background. Even volunteers had to abide by the paperwork rules. He worked methodically on the form, filling in his educational and work experiences, using fiction where facts eluded him. But his mind was on something else.

If he leaned forward just a little bit, he could get a clear view of Maggie at the front desk, her golden hair falling in a silken curtain as she bent over the accounting books she was checking out. It was a view he treated himself to more and more often, until the form was forgotten and enjoying Maggie was all he was doing.

She reached up to push the hair back behind her ear as he watched, revealing more of her pretty face. Glancing into the office, she met his steady gaze, and her lips parted before she smiled.

He smiled back, but she looked away quickly and shifted her position, determined to get on with her work. That made him grin. He wanted her. Desire curled like a lazy puff of smoke in his belly, and he didn't do anything to stave it off. A few seconds of it and his heart was beating faster, anticipating.

It had never been this way before, at least not any time he could remember. The urge to make love to a woman usually came on him suddenly, just before the fact, and was over quickly as soon as the need was fulfilled. But this was different, a slow, building heat that filled him like a drug and at the same time a quick, tearing excitement that reminded him of how he felt at the start of a race.

"You got that done yet?" Burt's sharp tone brought him back to reality with a lurch.

David glanced over at the older man, bemused by his seeming change of heart. Every other time they'd met, the man had acted like his biggest fan, but now his creased face was full of suspicion and resentment.

"Not quite," David replied dryly. He watched Burt carefully, seeing the older man's gaze wander over to Maggie, then turn away again.

So that was it. David almost laughed aloud. Burt wanted Maggie for himself? But no, he realized right away it wasn't that. This was fatherly interest. Another gallant man hoping to avert a broken heart for beloved Maggie.

Annoyance sliced through him. What did they all think, that he was Bluebeard or something? He'd never knowingly hurt anyone in his life. He thought of Mark's angry face and sighed. He'd lived all over the country, but this was without a doubt the most parochial small town he'd ever been in. Oh well, in just a few months he'd be gone. In the meantime he meant to enjoy himself. And give Maggie a good time, too, if possible.

"Here you go." He stood and handed the completed form to Burt. "Now you know all there is to know about me."

Burt grunted but didn't look up.

"See you tomorrow," David said cheerfully, and he left the room, stopping at Maggie on his way. "See you tonight," he added softly.

She looked up, her eyes wide and trusting. "Tonight," she repeated, and it was a promise they both understood.

For just a second David found himself hesitating. Those clear, honest eyes . . . Lord but he wanted her. He would do just about anything to be with her. She wasn't his type, he knew that. She was much too vulnerable, and he should leave her alone. But it was too late. He couldn't.

But instead of feeling guilt, suddenly he felt something else—a vague sense of wariness. Did he know what he was doing here? Had he really weighed the risks he was taking? Was he passing beyond a point of no return?

David shrugged the warning off. He could handle the situation. He gave Maggie a grin and turned to leave the building. He was letting the small-town prudes and values get under his skin. She was something he wanted, and he was going to have her. There was no problem. None at all.

CHAPTER SEVEN

The doorbell rang, and Maggie groaned. Another interruption. She'd counted on a full hour of free time to get ready for her date with David, and so far she hadn't had a second to spare.

First her mother had called her at work, asking that she stop at the farmers' market to pick up a head of lettuce for her father's dinner. At the market she'd run into Grace Holmes, her ninth-grade science teacher, who'd insisted on getting caught up on what Maggie had been doing with herself lately. Then, finally home, her neighbor had come running over to ask Maggie to take care of her three children while she raced out to help her husband with a flat tire he'd had ten miles out of town.

"The spare is just as flat as a pancake, Carl says. He called me on the CB. I won't be gone long," Janey had promised. "But I hate to take the babies out there in a hot car while we work on the tire. And you're always telling me how you'd like to have them for a while."

It was true. Maggie adored the five-month-old twins, as well as their four-year-old brother Cory. Normally she would have welcomed a chance to have them to herself for half an hour. But not tonight.

Tonight she'd wanted to soak in a hot bubble bath, pour fragrant oils all over herself, then spend another fifteen minutes curling her hair just right. Twenty minutes devoted to trying on different dresses seemed about right, picking the exact one sure to bowl David over. Instead—diapers and formula. And now there was someone at her door.

"Just a minute," she called, looking down at Libby and Larry, the two babies in her arms. Cory was bedded down in the hall closet—his favorite place whenever he dropped in for a visit, since she sometimes hid toys she'd bought for him there. Cory was easy. He played with his miniature cars and trucks, or curled up in the coats and slept. But the twins were another matter, for they demanded constant attention.

Right now Libby was giving off signs of needing to be changed. Dropping to her knees, Maggie deposited the little girl in the middle of the changing cloth she'd spread out on the floor, then rose with Larry still in her arms and hurried to the door, pulling it open.

Dressed in gray slacks and a soft blue sweater that hugged his body like a caress, David stood before her looking gorgeous and irresistible—and yet he was definitely not a welcome sight.

"You're early!" Maggie wailed, conscious of her mussed hair and the same wrinkled clothes she'd been wearing all day.

His smile was slow and seductive as he leaned against the doorjamb, the embodiment of all she'd ever dreamed of, like some sexy, romantic hero from an old-fashioned movie, so near and yet so totally out of reach. "I couldn't stay away," he said huskily, completing the image.

Maggie began to melt. The promise in his deep, dark eyes was enough to make her forget everything else. But she didn't get to enjoy more than a second or two before reality took over again.

A sudden shriek from the angry baby in the bedroom wiped the suggestive look right off David's face.

"Who's that?" he asked, looking alarmed.

Maggie felt disaster at her doorstep, but there wasn't much she could do about it. Why had David picked this particular time to show up early? "You may regret this," she warned, throwing the door wide open.

And that was when David noticed the baby on her hip. "What is *that?*" he asked suspiciously, edging around her as he came in the door. He obviously had no intention of getting too close.

Maggie felt frazzled. The screams emanating from the bedroom were getting louder and more insistent, and each one seemed to tear another hole in the fabric of the picture she'd imagined tonight would be. She looked at David with a mixture of resentment and helplessness. Why when it was so patently time for things to start going right in this relationship did things have to go so very, very wrong? It wasn't David's fault, but there was no one else to blame at the moment.

"It's a baby," she snapped. "Here, hold him." She thrust her tiny bundle into his hands. "I'll be right back."

David took the baby as though he were afraid it might be carrying a communicable disease, his gaze following

Maggie anxiously as she left the room. "What do I do with it?" he called after her.

"Be creative," she called back. "What do you usually do with children?"

He'd never held a child before—and he'd never really planned on holding one, either. Still, he had to do *something*. The baby was beginning to wriggle around as if he were thinking of launching a flight pattern from David's arms. David eyed him with distrust. Perhaps a little conversation . . . "Does he talk?" he asked loudly.

"Of course not," Maggie called back.

That about exhausted his ideas. He pulled back the blanket so he could get a better look at the little pushed-in thing he supposed must be its face. He stared down at it. It looked like a strange being from another planet, a pink and white blob, some kind of weird life form that he'd never come this close to before.

"Then what am I supposed to do with him?"

"I don't know. Wave a rattle at him. Sing him a song."

"Sing," he muttered. He held the baby awkwardly, swaying back and forth the way he'd seen people do in movies, but it didn't feel right. "I can't carry a tune, how'm I going to sing?"

He tried to hum, but the results weren't good. As he watched, the tiny lower lip suddenly began to tremble.

The kid was going to cry. David sighed. He had to do something. Somehow he suspected that a good solid shake would probably be against baby-union rules. Maybe the little tyke would respond to talking after all, if it was done right?

"Hello," he said a bit formally, nodding down at

Larry. "How are you this evening? Nice weather, don't you think?"

The tremble escalated to an outright whimper. There was a look of terror in the baby's eyes, and they rolled around searching for an escape from this horrible monster of a man who talked in a low voice and held him so stiffly.

David clutched the baby more tightly, feeling almost desperate. Suddenly he was determined not to be humiliated as a baby-sitter. "Hey, don't do that. I just want to talk to you."

A slight sound from behind him caught his attention and he turned just in time to catch a small redheaded figure peering out from around the hall closet door. David stared. Two blue eyes stared back.

"You're holding him wrong," the little boy said at last.

"What?" David looked down at his bundle.

"You gotta hold his neck or he'll go brain damaged."

"Oh, I see." David hastily put a hand out to support what there was of the stubby little neck. "Is that how?"

The little boy nodded solemnly and disappeared back into the closet.

Before David had a chance to react, Maggie came bustling back into the room, holding another version of the figure David was carrying around with him. "Here, let me take him," she said, reaching for the squirming child in David's arms. "Can you hold Libby for a minute? I just changed her. I'd better change Larry, too."

"Two of them," David muttered, making the exchange. He eyed Maggie speculatively. She hadn't mentioned where these babies had come from. "Some people don't know when to stop."

But Maggie wasn't paying any attention. She was concentrating on the warm little package in her arms. "Oh sweetheart, don't cry," she cooed, and as the baby realized he'd been transferred to the protection of someone who knew what she was doing, the crying did stop. Little Larry beamed up at Maggie, then craned his little neck to smile back at David—a bit smugly, David thought with resentment.

Maggie looked up at David too. He noticed how distracted she was, how totally devoid of interest in him at the moment, and he felt a twinge of jealousy. Maggie was a baby person, that much was clear. What was she running here, a nursery? They couldn't possibly be hers, could they?

"Just hold Libby for a minute," she said, turning away. "I'll be right back."

"Do I have to? They don't like me."

Maggie heard the note of quiet desperation in his voice and she stopped, turning back. "Oh David, I'm so sorry about this. But we'll get them to sleep in a few minutes." She smiled encouragement. "Anyway, they'll like you just fine once they get to know you. Sit down on the couch and just rock her a bit."

David looked at the little face in his arms as Maggie left him alone again. "Maybe I don't want you to get to know me," he whispered, but not loud enough for Maggie to hear. Libby stared up at him. There was no feeling of instant friendship evident at all. Instant enmity was more like it. Libby didn't even bother to start with the trembling lip. She went right into screaming at the top of her lungs and David sighed, dropping down on the couch as Maggie had suggested.

"Don't they come with plugs?" he asked in a voice loud enough to rise above the din. "Little rubbery things that fit into their mouths?"

"You mean pacifiers," she called from the bedroom. "Janey doesn't believe in them."

He rocked his bundle, patting it awkwardly. "Who's Janey?"

"Their mother."

He rocked harder, in time with the screams. "You mean they're not yours?"

She stuck her head back in the room. "Be serious." She saw the look on his face and realized he was only half-teasing. "You didn't really think they were mine?"

He shrugged, holding the baby up against his shoulder in another effort to stifle the crying. "I didn't know. But the idea was certainly scary."

She laughed, wanting to go to him, but Larry began to squeal and she hurried back.

"It's just you and me, kid," David muttered consolingly to Libby, but the baby just screamed louder. "I could take her for a ride on my motorcycle," he called in to Maggie. "That might quiet her down."

"Don't you dare!"

"Why not? The breeze in her hair, a few gnats in her teeth . . . She'd love it."

"She doesn't have enough teeth for gnat catching."

"Details," David muttered.

The telephone rang, adding to the symphony of sound that was destroying his eardrums.

"Could you get that?" Maggie called from the bedroom.

"I could if I had three hands," David grumbled, but only to the baby and himself. He sidled over to the table and picked up the phone on the fourth ring. Libby hiccupped in his arms and went quiet, as though she wanted to listen in on the conversation herself.

"Hello," David said.

There was a pause. "I must have the wrong number," said a deep voice. "Is Maggie there?"

A male caller. David's competitive instincts were immediately aroused. "Who's calling?"

"Bill Smith."

The notorious Bill Smith. For just a moment he toyed with the idea of telling him Maggie had joined a convent or left for mountain climbing in Tibet, but something told him the ploy wouldn't work. But there were other ways to handle this. "Just a moment. I'll see if she can come to the phone." He clamped the receiver to his chest. "Maggie, it's for you."

"Ask them to call back later," she said, sounding flustered. "Like tomorrow."

David smiled and put the receiver to his mouth. "I'm afraid she can't take your call right now," he said smoothly. "You see, Maggie and I are putting the babies to bed. Try again tomorrow, why don't you?"

There was a long, awkward silence. "Babies?"

"That's right. Maggie's a fast worker." Libby gurgled in his arms. "They're twins. Double trouble, and all that.

Some say they look like their mama, some say they look exactly like their dad. But who cares? They're both a couple of cuties."

"Are—are you sure this is Maggie Jones's number?"

David's laugh was short. "Are you kidding? Would I be putting babies to bed at any other Maggie's house?"

Bill was finally suspicious. "Who is this?"

"David, who else? Well, gotta go. Duty calls."

He put the telephone down and smiled happily, picturing Bill staring at the receiver in total confusion. Sitting down, he grinned at Libby and bounced her on his knee.

"Who was it?" Maggie asked, bustling out into the living room.

"Bill. I told him you were busy having babies."

"Mm, good," she said absently. "What's that wet spot on your slacks?"

David was suddenly aware of a warm feeling where none had existed just seconds before. "Oh—!"

"Don't swear in front of the children," Maggie interrupted, then laughed ruefully. "Time to change her again."

"How about me? Got any diapers in my size?"

"Hold Larry. I'll bring you back a damp cloth."

"Wait a minute—what is this, musical babies?" He took Larry, but this time he followed Maggie into the bedroom and watched while she changed Libby's diaper.

"Look," Maggie exclaimed as she worked. "They're all red in the face from all that crying. If they're like that when their mother comes to get them, she'll never let me take care of them again."

"Go for it, I say."

Maggie glared at him. "Hand me the powder, please."

"Are you going to tell me where these little beauties came from?"

Maggie grinned. "Didn't anyone ever explain the birds and the bees to you?" she asked archly.

He gave her a heavy-lidded stare. "No one's ever accused me of being ignorant in that department," he countered. "What I want to know is what particular stork left these little guys on your doorstep."

She explained about Janey and the flat tire. "She ought to be back any minute." Glancing at her bedside clock, she gasped. "Oh no. She should have been here ages ago. I wonder what's happened."

David looked down at Larry, whose lower lip was trembling again. "I'm beginning to get a bad feeling about this," he told him. Larry took that as his cue to howl. David sighed, giving Maggie a look of pure disgust. "And people actually live with these things."

"Yes, people do. And quite happily, too. I'm planning to have a few of them myself."

"Before or after they lock you away in the asylum?"

He left the room rather hurriedly, just in case Maggie decided to throw something at his head.

Little Larry was in fine voice once again. David felt like a condemned man. He rocked the baby, tried to talk to it, waved a rattle; nothing worked. Sing, Maggie had said. " 'Oh beautiful, for spacious skies, for amber waves of grain . . .' " he began.

The closet door opened again. The same two blue eyes looked out.

"He hates that song," the little boy informed David

solemnly. "He only likes 'Little Toot' when I sing it to him."

David smiled hopefully. "Would you like to come sing it to him now?"

"No."

"But I don't know 'Little Toot.' "

The closet door pulled shut and the blue eyes disappeared.

"Thanks a lot," David muttered. The howls were driving him crazy. He looked down at the red-faced child and sighed. " 'Little Toot,' " he said experimentally.

The screams came to an abrupt halt and Larry's little eyes peered up at him expectantly.

"Toot, toot, tootledy toot," David went on. The little mouth opened in a yawn and the little eyes seemed to drift shut. It was actually working. Feeling quite pleased with himself, he rocked Larry and tooted into his ear, watching him slowly fall asleep.

Mission was almost accomplished when Maggie came back into the room and destroyed his satisfaction. "Oh, don't let him go to sleep," she cried the moment she spotted what he was doing.

David's face took on a haggard expression. "Why on earth not?"

She put Libby into the portable crib against the wall, propped her with a bottle of juice and turned back to get Larry. "If he sleeps now, he'll never sleep through the night."

He supposed there was some sort of logic to that, but not any he was interested in. He watched as Maggie took Larry from him and put him in the crib with his sister.

"Did you know there's a short person living in your closet?" he asked casually.

"Hmm?" Her face paled, and she straightened from her work in the crib. "Oh, Cory. I'd forgotten all about him!"

"You know him, then?"

"He's the twins' brother." She pulled open the closet door. "Hi, Cory. You okay in there?"

Cory nodded from the bed he'd made for himself among the fallen coats and sweaters.

"All right. Your mother should be home soon."

She closed the closet door and turned to fling herself down on the couch beside David. "I hope," she whispered to him.

"If she's smart she's run off to Madagascar to join the revolution. It would be more peaceful than what she must be used to here."

"This?" Maggie grinned at him. "This was nothing. We didn't even have to feed them."

He looked at the two little tyrants, each drinking eagerly from the bottles Maggie had provided. "All you're doing is revving them up for more diaper changes," he complained. "It's an endless cycle."

"Like life," she agreed.

Not like *his* life. He looked at her, so close beside him on the couch. She was mussed, but sexy as any woman he'd ever seen. Part of him wanted to reach out and take her in his arms, but another part was still getting used to thinking of her as an earth-mother type. Earth mothers weren't fair game. They didn't fit into his life-style.

Maggie saw the question in his eyes, and though she

wasn't sure just what it meant, she could sense his hesitation. Confused, she rose and went to the babies. They, at least, were easy to understand. Their wants and needs were issued at the top of their lungs. They didn't have ambivalent feelings about anything. She could respond when she knew what was needed. The way David looked at her, she didn't know what to do.

Watching her, David felt restless, uneasy. Maggie disturbed him, the babies disturbed him. And why not? This was a night of firsts for him. He'd never been forced to deal with real live babies before. These were, after all, the obvious products of liaisons between men and women. He'd always been aware of them, theoretically, but this was the first time he'd come face to face with the reality. This was why people made love—to get these little squirming squishy things. It put a whole new light on the subject for him. To think of what he'd been risking all these years!

He had to admit the little pink blobs felt kind of nice after he got used to them, but the noises they made were the pits. Still, looking across the room to where Maggie leaned over Larry, cooing softly and coaxing him to drink his bottle, he felt an unaccustomed tug at his heartstrings. What a pretty picture they made. Maggie was obviously a natural-born mother.

"And I," he muttered beneath his breath, "am a natural-born fool."

It was almost an hour before Janey arrived at the door. Finally the twins were packed off safely to their cribs and Cory was led, eyes scarcely open, down the hall to his own bed, leaving David and Maggie alone.

Maggie turned to him, smiling shyly. The apartment seemed suddenly so quiet, but signs of chaos still littered the floor and the furniture. She wasn't sure just how much he'd hated it all. Was there any romance left in him? "I could go change," she offered, looking down at her rumpled clothes.

He shook his head. Reaching out, he lifted her chin with his hand. "No, Maggie," he said softly, gazing into her eyes. "You must be starved. Let's go out and grab a hamburger somewhere."

There was puzzlement in her eyes, but also a measure of relief. "Okay, if that's what you want."

It wasn't what he wanted at all. But for once he decided he was going to be one of the good guys. Rack up a few points. They went for hamburgers and sat across a booth from one another, talking until the cleaning staff came banging in with their mops and pails, and then they drove home and sat outside her apartment building for another hour, still talking.

Maggie talked about the only Christmas she'd spent away from home during her college days and about the time she broke her arm playing softball, and David told her about carnival in Rio de Janeiro and the time he went deep-sea fishing with Burt Reynolds. They'd led such different lives, yet Maggie was surprised to find how easy it was to talk to David. He was interested in anything and had a story about everything. He made her laugh, and he listened just as well as he talked. When she glanced at her watch and saw that it was three in the morning, she was stunned.

He walked her to her door, and she turned with the

key in her hand, inviting him in. When he shook his head, bent to kiss her softly on the lips and then headed down the hallway, she could hardly believe it. Despite all of what he'd said, all his warnings, they really weren't going to make love. Bewildered, she watched him walk off down the corridor, and then she slipped into her lonely apartment and went to bed all alone.

The next few days proved to be more of the same. David came to the Youth Center every afternoon to work with the boys, and they seemed to be making progress. He talked to Maggie, smiled at her, touched her now and then in passing. But he said nothing more about seeing her after work. Now and then she caught a look from him, sensed a hint of the fiery yearning that she'd felt so often before, but when she would try to get closer, he would turn away, his gaze hooded, his face blank.

Maggie didn't know what to do about it. She still felt the same. Her pulse raced when she first saw him every day, and the sound of his voice on the telephone made her tingle. Yet he was acting as though there could never be more between them than a laugh and a handshake.

"You're acting cuckoo," Cathy told her impatiently as they sat over hot fudge sundaes in the coffee shop one Saturday afternoon. "Like a lovesick cocker spaniel. Believe me, you're a disgusting sight these days."

"I'm not lovesick," she protested, but Cathy knew her too well.

"It's the motorcycle rider with the cute buns, isn't it? I heard he was working with you at the Youth Center these days."

Maggie glared at her friend. "Cathy, would you mind your own business?"

Cathy waved her sundae spoon. "See? I knew it was him. So what's the problem? He won't give you a tumble?"

Maggie's face went blank. "Did you see that new rack of dresses at Florence's shop yet? She goes right over to San Francisco to pick them out."

Cathy groaned. "All right, don't tell me. I'll see for myself when I come over for Burt's birthday on Monday."

Cathy's latest job was as a singing telegram, and Maggie had hired her to bring Burt a birthday message. Now she was afraid she was going to regret it.

"Cathy . . ." she began warningly.

Cathy threw up her hands. "Oh, don't worry for a second. I'll be discreet."

Discreet had never been a word used to describe Cathy before, and Maggie had some legitimate doubts. But Monday came and Cathy arrived, dressed like a can-can dancer and doing a spirited rendition of "The Way We Were," dancing while she sang—and it all went off very well. Everybody loved the performance and Cathy was invited to join them for cake and ice cream and a lot of loving toasts. Maggie caught her eyeing David speculatively now and then, but she didn't do anything outrageously embarrassing.

It was later that evening, when Maggie dropped in at Cathy's apartment for coffee and a chat, that Cathy delivered up her judgments.

"Aunt Cathy knows all, Aunt Cathy sees all," she announced, sitting cross-legged on the floor of her sparsely furnished room. "Listen, the guy is absolutely crazy about you."

Maggie's laugh was rueful. *"You're* the one who's crazy."

"No, listen to me. I know what you're thinking. The man is a total fox. He's got the come-hither eyes, the gorgeous bod, the knock-em-dead smile. He can just about crook his little finger and get any woman he wants. Right?"

Maggie set down her coffee mug and eyed it with distaste. "That sounds like a fairly accurate portrait," she said between gritted teeth.

Cathy leaned forward, eyes shining. "But he wants you. And he's scared to get you."

Startled, Maggie stared at her.

"Don't you see? He's decided you're the virginal type."

"What?" Maggie had to laugh. "No, I don't think so—"

"Oh, it's true. I could see it right away. He's shoved you up on a pedestal and now he thinks you're up there in the clouds somewhere and he doesn't deserve you." She grinned, pleased with her own diagnosis. "You've got to show him otherwise. And don't be subtle. Men aren't awfully perceptive. I should know!"

Maggie didn't really believe a word Cathy was saying, but the theory intrigued her nonetheless. "You mean, I should take the initiative—"

"Absolutely." Cathy's eyes blazed with excitement. "Listen, I really have access to a lot of things with the telegram job. Like costumes. What you need is a sexy dress, cut low in front and high over the thigh. One of those dresses with the feather borders all around. And black mesh stockings. And a good dousing of Delirium perfume."

"I don't need any of those things," Maggie said dreamily.

Cathy jumped up, annoyed. "Of course you do. Good props are half the battle."

Maggie reached for her bag and pulled out a piece of paper, waving it at Cathy. "His roster," she said. "He left it at the office tonight, and I have a feeling he's going to need it at the trials competition tomorrow."

"Well, sure, but—"

"I'm going over to his apartment right now," Maggie said decisively. "Before I lose my nerve."

"But you're not ready! You need a sexy dress—"

Maggie looked down at her jeans and white cotton sweater. "He'll have to take me as I am," she said firmly. "And if he thinks this is virginal, I'll just have to show him different."

"Atta girl!" Cathy followed her to the door. "Go get him, tiger!"

At the last minute Maggie turned back slowly and held Cathy's gaze with her own. "Are you really sure about all this?" she asked softly.

Cathy's gaze wavered. "Well, no," she admitted. "But it's worth a shot. He's a hunk."

Maggie laughed. On impulse she went back and gave Cathy a big hug, then went down to the parking lot, still laughing. Cathy was right. It was worth a shot. She only hoped she didn't end up shooting herself in the foot.

CHAPTER EIGHT

Maggie spent almost half an hour parked on the street in front of David's apartment building before she worked up the nerve to go to his door. She knew which apartment it was and she could see that the light was on, but a thousand possibilities swarmed in her mind—all of them bad.

What if he didn't answer the door? Wouldn't she feel like a fool out there pounding away? What if he had a bunch of friends over for a poker game? Wouldn't she be embarrassed? What if he had a woman in there with him?

That was the worst one. Every time she thought about it her stomach seemed to drop away, as though she were on a roller coaster, sitting in the very front seat. After all, David was extremely attractive to women, and from all indications there was no shortage of eager companions for him. Why wouldn't he have a woman up there? What did she think, that he was waiting in his apartment for Maggie Jones to drop in some night?

With an unhappy sigh Maggie forced herself to leave the protection of her car for the terrifying unknown of David's apartment.

She knocked instead of ringing. Somehow that seemed more personal. And she was feeling very personal.

He opened the door, but not all the way. "Maggie." He looked surprised to see her. His hair was tousled, as though he'd been wrestling with a tough problem, and his eyes looked tired. He wore jeans and a cut-off sweatshirt that exposed his muscular arms and strong, corded neck.

Maggie was proud of herself. She plastered a blithe, friendly smile on her face and acted as though there were nothing at all unusual about her showing up at his doorstep. "You forgot this at the Youth Center this evening." She held out the roster. "I thought I'd bring it by."

He looked at it for a moment, then took it from her. "Thanks," he said, his gaze steady but unrevealing. "But I've got another copy here. You didn't have to make a special trip."

She shrugged. "Well, I thought, with the special practice tomorrow and all . . ." Her voice trailed off. He wasn't being a bit welcoming. He still hadn't opened his door all the way. Did that mean that he had someone else in there? Part of her wanted to make a run for it and never find out, but another part wanted to know for sure.

"Thanks," he said again, his eyes hooded. "I'd ask you in, but my place is a mess, and—"

"I don't mind messes." Stunning even herself with her boldness, she pushed at the door, forcing him back, and made her way in around him. Her gaze darted from one corner of the room to another. No evidence of anyone yet. Could she be hiding in the bathroom? "I wanted to talk to you, actually."

She turned and dared herself to look him in the eyes. They were deep and filled with mystery. Was he angry? She looked toward the still-open front door, then back at him. "Can we talk?" she asked brightly, though her spirits were flagging.

He shifted his weight from one foot to the other, a frown on his handsome face. "Why don't we go out and get something to eat?" he suggested. "We could talk in the restaurant."

He was still trying to get rid of her. A thread of despair made its way up her throat and she turned away, her gaze sweeping over the room. It was starkly furnished—a television, a bookcase, a couch, two chairs, a table. And on the table a half-empty bottle of Scotch. Next to it, a full glass. Only one glass. He was alone.

Relief surged through her. She looked at him, her smile trembling a bit around the edges.

The vulnerability in her face hit him like a slap, and he was beside her in an instant, his arm supporting her. "What's wrong? Are you all right?" His voice was rough, but his concern was obvious.

Maggie shook her head, not knowing what to say, where to go from here. "I—I'm fine. It's just . . ." Her laugh sounded strained. "Do you know I've never gone to a man's apartment before? Alone, I mean. Without being asked first."

He glared down at her, his expression a mixture of exasperation and wariness. "Did you come for anything special?" he asked gruffly.

She backed away so that she could look into his face. "I came as a friend," she said slowly. "What do you usually do when a friend comes over? Give him the third degree? Or offer him a chair?"

Hesitating for just a moment, he gestured toward the

couch. "By all means, have a seat," he said with little hospitality.

She sat down gingerly on the edge of the cushion. "Thank you," she said brightly. "Now if you'd only look glad to see me."

The exasperation faded, but he still stood over her, his basic distrust clear in his expression. "Of course I'm glad to see you," he said shortly. "I'm always glad to see you." But he didn't look glad. "Can I get you anything?"

"Oh, yes. A drink." Wasn't that what they always said in movies when they needed moral courage? "I could really use a good, stiff drink." She glanced at the Scotch on the table and winced. "Do you have any white wine?"

David stared at her for a moment. Then his face broke into a reluctant grin and he covered it with his hand. "Maggie, Maggie," he murmured, shaking his head. "You're going to drive me crazy."

She had no idea what he meant. "If you don't have any wine. . . ."

He held out his hand. "No problem. I've got it." He left the room and returned almost immediately with a wineglass and a bottle of Chablis. He filled the glass with the silvery liquid and held it out to her. "Don't overdo it now," he said sternly, and only the sparkle in his eyes told her he was teasing. "We don't want any trouble."

He was making fun of her, but she didn't mind. It was so wonderful to have the harsh disapproval gone from his face. She took a long sip of wine and felt herself relax.

"Do you usually leave your door open like that?" she asked, gesturing at the doorway.

He didn't grin this time. He looked from her to the

door, then strode across the room and closed it. When he came back he hesitated for a moment between the chair and the couch and finally chose the latter, sitting about a foot away from Maggie.

"That was a nice birthday surprise you planned for Burt today," he said casually, making conversation.

She took another sip of wine and smiled brightly. "Cathy was cute in her ruffled dress, wasn't she?"

David nodded. "I take it she's a good friend of yours?"

"The best. We've been friends all our lives."

He nodded again, then raised an eyebrow. "What is she to your brother Mark?"

"Mark?" Maggie looked puzzled. "Mark wasn't there today."

"I know. But Cathy must have mentioned him fifty times."

"Oh." Maggie dismissed his comment with a wave of her hand. "They've always been friendly adversaries. She loves to bug him."

"I see." He moved restlessly. "How's Bill these days?"

"Bill?" She looked at him in surprise. "I don't know. I haven't seen him in ages."

He laughed shortly. "What happened to the wedding plans?"

"Wedding plans?" She frowned in confusion, then remembered why he might ask such a thing. "Oh. No, that was sort of a mistake. We—we aren't getting married. We never really were."

"Oh."

But he didn't even look happy to hear the news. That bit of conversation petered out, and they sat staring at the wall. There didn't seem to be any other small talk left between them. But there was something there, something pulsing and twisting, something that wouldn't leave either one of them alone.

"Okay," David said at last. "You wanted to talk. What did you want to talk about?"

She looked at him and all her courage fell away. What could she say to him? Why don't you smile at me the way you used to? Why do you make a point of not touching me when we pass each other in the halls? Why did you promise me so much and give me so little?

Impossible. She couldn't say it right out that way. She'd have to find a more roundabout way.

"I don't know quite how to put this . . ." she began.

He looked away as though he didn't know how, either, and wished she wouldn't bring it up at all. Well, perhaps she wouldn't. She took a long drink of her wine, then set down her glass and stood, beginning to pace about his room, stopping to look at a landscape on the wall, a pair of shells on the bookcase, a model of a motorcycle on the television set. "Don't you have any photographs?" she asked thoughtlessly.

"Photographs?" He seemed to stiffen.

"Photos. Of yourself, girlfriends, high school days—whatever."

"No photos." His dark eyes followed her movement around the room, but he remained perfectly still.

She turned to look at him. "Don't you like being reminded of your past?"

His face darkened. "I have no past, Maggie," he said softly. "I live for today, not yesterday."

The words sounded so cold. No past. How could that be? To Maggie, life was half the past all intertwined with the present and hopes for the future. How could you know who you were without a past?

He was so very different from her and all she was used to, so disconnected, so cool—an outsider, an observer. She didn't belong here. And yet she knew she wouldn't go away of her own free will. She pushed the hair back from her face and looked around, knowing she should sit down but too nervous to do so. Instead she walked over to look into the kitchen.

"Nice," she commented. "Neat and clean. Did you do this?"

He stood and came up behind her. "I'm a neat and clean guy," he said quietly and without a trace of irony. "Didn't you know that?"

She turned and looked at him. He stood a few feet away, and Maggie's heart started beating very fast. She stared at him for a moment, then took two quick steps to the other door.

"Is this your bedroom?" she asked, peering in.

"Yes." He'd come up behind her again. She shivered with his nearness. "Why?"

"I just want to see where you sleep."

"Why?"

She glanced at him, then away. How could she explain that she wanted to know everything about him, touch everything that he touched. The lamp wasn't on in his bedroom, but there was enough light from the living room to lessen the gloom.

The bed was nicely made, but once again the walls and

shelves were stark, with hardly anything personal showing. *Where was the real David Duke hiding,* she wondered? Why was he so reluctant to show himself?

"No teddy bear?" she quipped.

"No teddy bear. No one at all, in fact."

She turned and looked up at him, so close, leaning with one hand flattened against the wall. The sense of him hit her with physical force and she wanted to grab hold of him, to pull him closer, to lose herself in the feel and the smell of him.

"What is it that you want, Maggie?" he asked, his voice husky.

You, she cried to him silently. Couldn't he read it in her eyes? "A stronger drink," she said aloud, tossing her hair back again. "Something hot and burning. May I try your Scotch?"

She started toward the table, but he grabbed hold of her wrist and stopped her. "You should go," he said simply, his eyes smoky with some rare emotion.

She tilted her face to his. "I don't want to go," she said breathlessly, her eyes full of challenge.

There was a knot in his stomach and it was tightening. Her wrist felt fragile in his hand. Hungrily he pulled her a little closer, his gaze sweeping across her tantalizing mouth, the curve of her cheek, the long, graceful line of her neck.

When he was very young he'd been denied everything a child should have—parents, a home, love, security. And since he'd grown old enough to chart his own destiny, he hadn't denied himself anything that he'd wanted. As if to make up for those painful years, he'd shown the world around him his power, taken what he desired, disregarded the rest. But Maggie—he'd decided to spare her. He wanted her like he'd never wanted another woman, and yet he'd told himself he was strong enough to resist her.

Still, there were limits.

"It's late," he told her hoarsely. "We can talk in the morning."

"Is it too late?" she asked, twisting his words, staring at the strong, dark fingers that held her. Now or never. Go for broke. The phrases echoed in her head, and she hardly knew what she was doing. Slowly she turned and reached out her hand, sliding it up under his short sweatshirt. His skin felt like satin, and she could feel him draw in a breath at her touch. Her fingers were trembling. "Is it really too late?"

The sweet, musky scent of her hair filled his nostrils, and a throbbing began in his head. His gaze lowered to the swell of her breasts, visible beneath the low V of her sweater. She was so close, and her body was pulling at him with a force that took his breath away.

"Maggie, Maggie," he murmured, half in despair. "If you stay, I'm going to make love to you."

She lifted her face to his, her eyes dreamy with longing. "What do you think I came for?" she whispered.

The throbbing seemed to fill him, burning inside. His free hand swept into her hair, fingers gripping harshly. "I can't promise you anything, Maggie. You were made for better things . . . a better man . . ."

"No I wasn't." Her gaze didn't waver. "I was made for you."

Groaning, he pulled her into his arms and she melted there, pliant, yet alive to his promise. The throbbing in his head was louder, more insistent, driving him on. He knew there would be no stopping now; his need for her was as deep and unremitting as the need for air. His mouth covered hers, capturing her greedily.

Her taste was dark, disturbing, and he drove deep, demanding more of her, delighting in her ready response. Despite the way he'd forced himself to view her, she wasn't acting like a shy virgin at all. She was a woman, ready and aware, as eager for the passion that was swelling between them as he was, making her own demands, revealing her own desire.

He pushed her sweater out of the way, and his hands stroked up and down her naked torso, first trailing a line of fire across her back, then sliding over her breasts, the fingers catching at the dark nipples, the palms stirring hot sensation. She sighed low in her throat, a deep, wanton sound that sent his equilibrium reeling.

He had to have her, had to have the ecstasy her body promised. And he had to make her feel it too. She was trembling and his hands were on the belt of her jeans, tearing at the closure, needing her now.

And then they were on his bed, and she was pulling at his leather belt, and he was shrugging out of his clothes and reaching for her at the same time. His hand went down the length of her, caressing, urging her to hurry, and she did, trembling eagerly in his arms.

"Golden girl," he whispered, his voice ragged with his near loss of control. "Oh Maggie, sweet Maggie . . ."

This was good. This was right. The sureness of it

soared inside him. They were good together, and if it worked here, why not always? He'd never needed anyone the way he needed her. She was so special, so right. She made him happy in a way he'd never been before. He couldn't lose her, and he would show her, show them both, how right it was.

"Sweet Maggie," he whispered again. "Oh Maggie . . ."

The only sounds she made were low and wordless. She touched him and her eyes closed as she gave way to her ecstasy. She was ready for him, he could feel it in her quivering response, hear it in the sounds she made. He came atop her and she opened her eyes wide, waiting, breath held, then crying out as he slid inside her. The hungry tide overwhelmed her immediately and she cried out again and again, lost to dignity, to civilization, completely won over by the primitive urge that wouldn't die away.

And even when it seemed finally to be over, David let go of his shaky control at last and it began again, wave after wave, carrying her to a mindless oblivion that went beyond pleasure to a shuddering rapture she could never have imagined to exist.

Spent with passion, Maggie lay very still. She didn't want to open her eyes in case it turned out to be a dream. She knew her life had changed. After this, everything would be different. She would be held by him as surely as the moon was held by the pull of the earth. No matter where he went or what he did, the hold would be there.

No, it wasn't a dream. She could feel him lying beside

her, hear his ragged breathing. He was real. She reached out a hand and curled it inside his. He was hers.

David rose on his elbow to watch her in the dim light. Her skin looked warm and rich as liquid honey, her hair a mass of golden light. Her eyes were dark smudges on a face that had etched a place in his memory. When he looked at her, feelings welled up inside him, feelings that shook him to his core.

Just moments before he'd been so sure this was right. But he hadn't been thinking clearly. Because it was wrong, so wrong.

And yet, looking at her, how could he tell himself that he regretted what had just happened? No strings, no entanglements—he'd always sworn that. He'd known what it was like to yearn for human bonding and not get it when it was most desperately needed. And so he'd sworn he would never need it again. He'd made himself strong enough to stand without the support of others, and for years it had worked just fine. Then this small-town waif had come into his life. And now here he was, needing her already, because this was different from anything he'd ever had before. Better. Deeper. Irresistible.

But that was all wrong. His mind recoiled at the concept. It was too dangerous to need anyone this badly. He had to find a way out.

He pulled away from her, staring at the wall. He would have to leave, go as far from here as he could get. He wouldn't write. He wouldn't call. To do either of those things would be to make promises he couldn't possibly keep. He would go hard and fast and wipe her from his memory.

But deep inside he knew it was already too late for that. In a crazy, terrifying way she was part of his life now and he would never be rid of her, even though he would surely leave her. And the sting of losing her would be with him always.

"David?"

He felt her hand on his back and he closed his eyes. Leave her? How could he think of such a thing? Not yet, not yet.

He turned, reaching out to smooth her hair away from her pretty face. "Tired?" he asked softly.

She shook her head, opening her eyes and smiling with wonder at the tenderness she saw in his face.

His fingers curled around her ear. What the hell, he thought, they had this time together. At least they had that.

He leaned down to kiss her cheek caressingly. "One year I rode on one of those raft trips on the Kern River," he said musingly. "It was in the spring. The runoff from the melting snow in the mountains made the river a raging torrent." He shook his head, remembering. "It was a wild ride. All you could do was hang on for dear life and hope you lived through it."

She stared at him, wondering what his point was.

"That's what making love to you is like," he told her, laughter sparkling in his eyes. "I ought to check myself out for broken parts. You're quite a trip."

Maggie flushed and looked away, but she couldn't help

smiling as he chuckled. He leaned close, pressing his lips to her throat and drawing in her love-mussed scent.

"I'm glad you came tonight, Maggie," he told her. "Stay with me."

"Do you mean . . . ?"

"I mean all night." His tongue flicked out to taste her sweet skin. "I mean for the next five months. Until I leave."

Five months. That was all that was left of his stay. She shuddered, holding her arms close over her breasts. David watched her closely. He'd brought it up on purpose, not wanting her to forget. Above all, he didn't want to hurt her.

"I'll stay tonight," was all she could promise for now. She smiled up at him. "You know what? You couldn't drag me away."

His hand stroked up and down her naked body. "Good," he whispered. "Because I have plans for us."

I love you, she thought, but she wouldn't say it out loud. He didn't want to hear it, he didn't want to know it.

She'd always wondered what love would be like, wondered how she would know it when it came. Now it was here and she had no doubts. Everything in her yearned for David. Everything in her cared for him and every part of his life—even the past he refused to face.

His touch began to burn, and she felt her body moving of its own volition. "Oh, David . . ."

"You didn't think I wanted you here just to sleep with me, did you?" he teased. "If that was all I wanted I really would get myself a teddy bear."

Desire would always be just below the surface with him. She turned toward him, accepting that, accepting everything about him. Wasn't that what love was all about?

CHAPTER NINE

"Maggie, what do you think?" Burt stood in the doorway of her office, his face perplexed. "The girls have just asked me if they could come along to that trials meet at Three Rivers." He shook his head, his brow furrowed. "What do you think?"

Maggie leaned back in her swivel chair and grinned at her boss. "The girls" meant her gymnastics team. The trials meet they wanted to attend would be the first time the Winners would test their mettle—and their new riding skills—against others in the area. The boys were nervous. The girls were excited. And David was practically beside himself with anticipation.

"They won't win anything," he'd told Maggie at least twenty times in the last few days. "But they'll get the experience they need. And Jed—well, he just might do more than that. I'm not counting on anything, mind you. But he just might." And a happy grin would crease his handsome face.

Maggie couldn't blame the girls for wanting to be in on the action. "I told Randi she would have to ask you about it," she told Burt. "I'm glad she did. I think it's a wonderful idea. The girls want to show support for all Youth Center teams, get more of a spirited, family feeling around here, and I agree. If they come to this meet, maybe the Winners will come to the next gymnastics exhibition, and then maybe they'll all come out to support the swim team, and it could go on and on."

Burt still looked doubtful. "Who's going to take care of them? David will have his hands full with the boys."

Maggie rose and crossed the office toward him. She knew what was really bothering him. He didn't want to put it into words, but it was there nonetheless. He loved his Winners, would do almost anything for them, but he was a realist and he knew they would be considered, by the girls' parents, at least, as being from the wrong side of the tracks. It was one thing to watch them pal around here at the Youth Center but another to take the two groups on an out-of-town trip together.

"It's only for the day. And I'll go with them," she promised, giving the bearlike man an affectionate hug. "I was planning to go anyway. I'll ride herd on the girls."

Burt looked only partly relieved. "If you're sure . . ."

"I'll take care of everything." She landed a loud kiss on his cheek and sent him on his way. "The Winners are going to live up to their name, you know," she called after him down the hall. "They'll need an audience to cheer them on."

The Winners were certainly improving. It had been over a month now since David had taken over the group. He'd taught them an awful lot, but even more than that, he'd given them a new source of hope. Maggie could see it in their eyes.

And what about her own eyes? she mused as she came back in and sat down at her desk. Could the people she loved see the changes there? Probably. In fact, she was sure of it.

"Your eyes are sparkling like you've got a secret," her mother had said just the other day. "Want to share?"

She only wished she could. She saw David every night now; he was the most important person in her life. And yet he still refused to go with her to meet her parents. She felt terribly guilty about that—and sad, too. She'd always shared with her family. Now something so wonderful had happened that she wanted to share it with the world, and yet if she couldn't bring him home, how could she tell her parents about him?

"What about Thanksgiving?" she'd asked David just yesterday. "We always have all sorts of people on Thanksgiving. Practically everyone in town who doesn't have anywhere else to go. You wouldn't have to come as my—my special friend. You could come as Mark's co-worker—"

"Forget it, Maggie." He'd said the words softly, holding her as he spoke, but they'd hurt all the same, as he'd known they would. But it was better that she understand. "I'm not a family man. I do all right by myself."

"You don't have to join the family. They won't shanghai you. We'll even let you go after dinner." She'd tried to say it as a joke, but the words fell pitifully flat.

"Families make me nervous," he'd said, his patience fading. "Listen, Maggie. This relationship is just you and me. If you're expecting more—"

"Oh, no," she'd reassured him quickly. "But what will you do on Thanksgiving?"

He shrugged. "Go out into the hills and find myself a great riding area. Don't worry about me. I can survive without turkey and dressing."

Turkey and dressing were hardly the point, but he knew that.

"Give him time," Cathy advised later when they discussed the situation. "He'll come around."

Maggie wasn't so sure. Still, Cathy had been right before. And was she ever proud of herself! She'd taken to whistling "Love Is a Many-Splendored Thing" whenever she saw Maggie. "Gee, do you think I should open a dating service?" she'd mused recently. "I seem to have a natural talent for this stuff."

"Stick to singing telegrams," Maggie had warned her. "If things go bad there, people will only throw rotten fruit. Failed romances tend to get uglier."

Not that her mind was on failure. She didn't allow herself to think about the future. Her outlook was relentlessly cheery. Even her brother Mark had given up trying to warn her off. "As long as he makes you happy," he'd said reluctantly. "I won't say another word."

Burt was the only one who seemed to have reservations, and every time Maggie saw the doubt in his face, she felt a flutter in her heart.

But most of the time she was walking on air. The night she'd gone to David's apartment, her world had changed. Her body was alive in ways it had never been before, and so was her mind. She was in love.

She sat at her desk now, staring at the purple and yellow flowers on the little plant that sat squarely in the middle of her working area. David had given it to her the day after they'd first made love.

"Here," he'd said carelessly. "These remind me of you. I went to get you red roses, but somehow when I saw these . . ." He smiled at her, his voice trailing off. "Red roses next time," he promised.

"African violets." She'd taken the plant in its gold foil wrapper and smiled. "I love them. But aren't they hard to grow?"

He shrugged. "No, not at all. They can last a long time, if you know how to nurture them right." He grinned. "At least that's what the lady at the plant shop told me."

She was trying hard. Just the right amount of watering, no drops on the fuzzy leaves, just the right amount of sunlight, just the right humidity. And so far everything was going well. The little flowers popped out and bloomed, a new bunch every few days. And every time she looked at them, she smiled.

Suddenly David was there, hitching a seat on the corner of her desk, grinning down at her. "Hey, lovely lady," he said softly. "Wanna neck?"

She threw her pen down and rose to slide her arms around him. There was no hesitation between them anymore. "I want a neck," she murmured, kissing his neck. "I want an ear." She gave that a peck. "And a nose—"

"Hey!" He held her off laughingly. "Leave a few body parts for me, okay? I just might need them someday."

"Selfish." She settled into his arms with a comfortable snuggle. "I want every part of you all to myself."

"Lock your office door," he whispered teasingly, "and I guarantee you'll have it all."

The harsh ring of her telephone ended that sweet dream. Laughing ruefully, she pulled out of his arms and picked up the receiver.

"Hello?"

"Hi, Maggie. It's Randi."

"Hello, Randi. I can't imagine what you could be calling for."

But the young girl didn't have time for teasing small talk. "What did he say? Is he going to let us go?"

Maggie smiled. "Yes, he'll let you go. As long as there are only four of you who are interested in going, you can ride up with me. Bring along lunches, and we'll stop on the way home for dinner. Okay?"

Randi's squeal of delight was the only answer she got, and once a chorus of squeals started up in the background, Maggie sighed and hung up. "It's all right with you if some of my gymnastics team comes along to the trials meet, isn't it?" she asked David as an afterthought.

"Sure, why not?" His face took on the intense look she was beginning to know so well. "They're ready, I know they are. If they just don't choke under pressure. . . ."

She slipped back into his arms. "Your boys will do beautifully," she reassured him.

" 'My boys'?" He repeated the phrase without the sarcasm he might have used a few weeks ago, more as though he was testing the sound of it. "Yeah, well, they've been working hard enough."

"And so have you. This will be a triumph. I can hardly wait to see it."

* * *

She should have known better, she told herself all Saturday afternoon. Overconfidence did it every time. If only they'd gone with lower expectations.

The trials competition was a disaster. Just about everything that could go wrong did. Two bikes refused to run. One of the boys got sick. Another got so frightened he refused to get on his motorcycle. The boys who did compete made major mistakes right from the beginning, disqualifying the entire team.

The atmosphere was terrific. It was warm for a November afternoon, the air full of dust and the sound of a hundred motorcycles revving up. People wandered in and out, looking over the competition. And behind it all was the roar of the river crashing through the boulders that had tumbled down from the Sierras.

"It is a great place for a picnic," Maggie said at one point, trying to look on the bright side. "The Keawah River, the sycamore trees . . ."

David's scowl killed the rest of her speech and she lapsed into worried silence, not sure what to do to alleviate the awful gloom that hung over their group.

The girls hardly noticed. It had quickly become obvious that they'd come to be with the boys, not to see any great motorcycle riding. In their own childish way they did what they could to cheer the boys up, and in a few cases it seemed to be working just fine.

But Maggie knew she wasn't going to be able to cheer up David. His face showed that he was closed to her right now. In fact, she had a feeling he would just as soon not have her there at all.

Actually he'd been good with most of the boys, patient and understanding when things had gone wrong. He'd held in his temper and explained where they'd made their mistakes, making each boy go back over what he'd done, pointing out the errors, assuring them that there would be other meets, other days. It was only with Jed Marker that he was as cold as ice. Watching the two of them together, Maggie felt a thread of unease.

But it wasn't until later, when she overheard a conversation between them, that his mood became clear to her.

She'd gone back to the van for another six-pack of sodas and had just reached out to pull open the sliding door when she heard voices on the other side of the vehicle. Stopping to see who it was, she heard David talking to Jed.

"Hey, man," Jed was saying defensively, "lay off. I did the best I could, okay?"

"No, Jed," David's voice responded with cold fury. "Not okay. You didn't even try out there."

Maggie stood frozen. She knew she should turn back and wait until this confrontation was over, but somehow she couldn't move.

"Listen, man, I got some problems at home, okay? My home life is kind of a bad situation. It's hard to concentrate on a bunch of stupid rules when you've got people messing up your mind all the time."

"So you're going to use that as your excuse to avoid life, are you?"

Jed sounded angry, too. "You don't know what I have to go through, man. You don't know—"

There was a sound, as though David had stepped forward to stop Jed from leaving. "You think I don't understand where you're coming from? You think you're the only one who didn't get born into a perfect world? Listen, Jed, I've been fending for myself since I was seven, and before that I didn't know who my father was and had only a vague idea of what a mother was supposed to be. I could have given up, too, and you know where I'd be today? Washing dishes to pick up booze money, maybe, or shooting up in an alleyway, getting beat up whenever any passing bum wanted something from me. Or in jail. Or dead. Instead I've got a good job, a good life and the opportunity to do anything I want with it. Freedom of choice. What you don't want to face is, you're never going to get out of that 'bad situation' unless you do something about it. Nobody else can do it but you. It takes guts and hard work. You don't seem to have the guts, and you sure as hell aren't willing to do the hard work. So where does that leave you? Right in the middle of that 'bad situation.' For the rest of your life."

"Hey, man, lay off, okay? I didn't ask for this. I'll find something—"

"No you won't. Life doesn't get better by taking the easy road. You didn't ask for this life, you didn't ask for this situation—but none of us did, did we? Where we start out is the luck of the draw. Where we end up is all in our own hands. Think about it. And when you're ready to take charge of your life, you come back and see me. I'm ready to help you all I can. But you've got to want it."

There was silence for a moment; then Jed spoke again.

"How come you're not telling the other guys this?" he asked resentfully.

"The other guys tried as hard as they could. You didn't."

"I made it further than any of them!"

"You should have made it all the way. You've got more potential in you than all the others put together. You've got it, Jed, but you're throwing it away. You've got what it takes to be one of the best. Maybe not in this. But in something."

"Like what?"

"Choose something, Jed. Choose something and learn how to work at it. Life is a prize, just hanging out there beyond your reach. You've got to make your grab for it. All you need is guts and work. Don't be afraid to try it. You've got nothing to lose."

From the sounds she heard Maggie could tell that Jed was walking off. She stood where she was. For the first time she was beginning to think she might one day understand David, understand why he was the way he was. Working hard, charting your own destiny—she'd always known he believed in those things. But the impetus behind his drive had been obscure to her until now. And though she still didn't fully understand it, she was closer than she'd ever been before.

David came around the van and frowned when he saw her standing there.

"I heard what you said to Jed," she told him without embarrassment. "I thought it was wonderful."

He ducked his head and began tinkering with one of

the motorcycles that was leaning nearby. "You weren't supposed to hear it."

"I know, but I did. And I want to say something to you, too." She crouched beside him, watching his deft hands move among the chrome parts. "Take your own advice, David Duke."

He looked up, eyes wide. "What?"

Her gaze was steady. "Take your own advice and come to Thanksgiving dinner with me and my parents."

"What?" The reluctance was clear on his face. He was so wary of families. Was that because his had let him down so badly? "I don't know what you're talking about. What does one thing have to do with the other?"

"Think about it," Maggie said, leaning over to kiss his cheek. "You don't have to say yes or no ahead of time. Just show up on Thanksgiving."

She rose and looked down at him. He went back to work without saying another word. She could feel the resistance in him as though it were a wall of steel. He didn't want to come. And when David didn't want to do something, it seemed almost beyond human power to make him do it.

Stradling his big black Honda, David slid the helmet over his head and fastened the strap. The air was cool and crisp, and there was a hint of frost. Not one cloud sullied the expanse of china-blue sky. He turned his gaze to the hills and waited. It didn't come.

Turning his face to the wind, he took in the heady fall fragrance of leaves burning, of pines, of clean winter snow from the mountains. But along with it he got a healthy dose of someone's pumpkin pies cooking, and he frowned, looking back at the hills. Why the hell didn't it come? It had always been there before—the quick rush of excitement, the tingling in his hands, the thrill of adventure beckoning to him from the great unknown trails waiting to be traveled.

Oh, well. If it wouldn't come to him, he would go to it. Kicking his motor into a roar, he sped off down the street, tires squealing as he took the curve at top speed. In moments he was out of town and heading out into the country. Mile after mile flew under his wheels. The hills loomed near. And still it didn't happen.

The hills, the great unknown, weren't beckoning to him as they always did. Instead something else was calling him. But fiercely he ignored the call and rode on.

He reached the hills, finding a rocky stream that wound up into a stand of aspen, a trail that tested him in exactly the way he wanted to be tested. He rode it, taking his motorcycle up and over rocks and logs that would have seemed impossible to cross to most riders. But his heart wasn't in it.

He found a lovely pond still circled by wildflowers. Stopping his bike, he switched off the engine and stared at the water. Why had he stopped, he wondered? What had compelled him to turn off the noise and be quiet for a moment, watching and listening?

You stopped, the answer came clearly, because you know Maggie would love it here.

He groaned, throwing back his head. "Damn it all to hell!" he yelled into the wilderness. And then he started his engine again with a vicious kick, and he rode right through the pond, splashing water everywhere.

Maggie loved the smells of Thanksgiving—the onions boiling, the candied sweet potatoes, the pies—and most of all, the turkey, browned to perfection, juicy inside.

The house was full of people. Sometimes it seemed as if everyone they knew showed up on this special day. "Remember why we're all here," said a banner her mother put up in the living room every year, "and give thanks."

"I'd give thanks for David," she whispered to no one in particular, "if he'd only show up."

It was getting late for that. Dinner was only about an hour away—and it was late this year because some out-of-town guests had only just arrived. She'd held on to the hope that he would change his mind and come, but hope was waning.

Deep inside, she knew that this did not portend well for her. As much as she told herself that he was a drifter, and that he was only hers for a short time, she couldn't help but hope for something more. When they were together, the love flowed between them like a lifeline that couldn't be severed. He'd never actually said he loved her, but she couldn't believe otherwise. How could he be so tender, so thoughtful, and not love her? He *had* to love her. And if he loved her, somehow he had to be convinced to stay.

He had a deep mistrust of close ties, but surely that was surmountable. If he would only come and meet her family, he would see they weren't so frightening. If he would only come . . .

"Can I taste the whipped cream?" Cory asked in a roar loud enough to be heard over the football game on the television in the next room.

"Of course not," Janey said sternly, testing the milk from a bottle against her wrist. "Wait until dessert." She strode quickly out of the room, a bottle in each hand.

Cory's face fell, and Maggie gestured for him to follow her to the refrigerator. "Here," she whispered, using the can to spray out a line of white foam on his finger. "Don't tell anyone."

Eyes huge, he nodded and ran off with his prize. Maggie looked up and saw Cathy laughing at her from the counter. "It's Thanksgiving," she said in her own defense.

"Did I say a word?" Cathy wanted to know, holding up her hands in mock innocence.

"Anyway, this is just for the decorating," Maggie went on, explaining when no explanation was needed as she put the can back in the refrigerator. "Mom's going to whip up fresh cream for the pies."

"See if Mom can whip up a little poison while she's at it," Cathy said, turning back to the chopping board to finish the celery. "I'd like to put a few drops in Sheila's toddy."

"Sheila?" Maggie looked at Cathy in amazement. Mark had brought Sheila to dinner, and the two of them were sitting out in the other room, talking to the houseful of guests. "What have you got against her? I think she's perfect for Mark."

"Why, because she doesn't say boo to anyone? Can't

you see? Mark needs someone lively, someone to pull him out of his sourpuss moods."

Maggie handed her an onion to chop along with the celery. "Well, I think Mark knows better than we do what he needs," she said musingly. "I thought you'd be happy for him. You've always been like a second sister to him—"

"A second sister!" Cathy threw down the knife, and Maggie turned to stare at her. Cathy's eyes were full of tears. "Onions," Cathy mumbled, and then she ran from the room. Maggie's gaze followed her.

"My goodness," she whispered aloud. "It can't be!"

But the more she thought about it, the more it added up. How could she have been so blind for so long? "Cathy is in love with Mark!"

Dropping everything she was doing, she followed her friend into the back bedroom, where she was sniffling into a handkerchief. "How long has this been going on?" Maggie asked softly, dropping down on the bed beside her.

Cathy's eyes were red. "Since junior high," she admitted.

Maggie threw an arm around her shoulders. "And you never said a word!"

"I knew I wasn't what you all were hoping Mark would find. You wanted a Sheila-type for him. But as long as he didn't go with anyone steadily, I hung in there. I was always around, just in case he might look up one day and notice me."

"Cathy!"

"But now there's this Sheila. I hate her! They've been going out for weeks."

"Oh, Cathy." Maggie didn't know what to do. She ached for her friend, but how could she help her? It was up to Mark to choose his own girlfriends.

"Don't worry about me." Cathy's chin rose. "I've done all right this long. I'll make out okay."

Before Maggie could answer, her mother appeared at the bedroom door. "There's someone here to see you, Maggie," she said, her eyes watching her daughter carefully. "A handsome young man."

Maggie jumped to her feet, flushing in spite of herself. "Is it—is it—?"

"He says his name is David Duke."

"Oh." Maggie's face said it all. Her mother didn't even have to ask.

"Why don't you come out and introduce him around?" she said gently. "I guess we'd all better get to know him."

The rest of the afternoon passed in a blur for Maggie. Faces came and went before her, and all she cared about was how David was reacting. To the innocent eye, he seemed to be doing quite well. He'd never had any trouble blending with people, and he didn't show any signs of being ill at ease here. He talked football with her father, talked gardening with her mother, played with the children. He did seem to blanch for a moment when he caught sight of the twins, but she had to hand it to him; he walked right up and took each chubby little hand in his.

"Hey, kids, remember me?" he said. "Don't cry now,

or I'll have to sing for you, and we all know where that leads."

Maggie tried to stand outside herself and judge how he would be seeing her parents. The more she tried, the more puzzled she became. There was nothing not to like about them. They were warm, friendly people, interested in him and in the world around them. What could possibly put him off about them? What could possibly be scary to a man like David?

David saw the way she was looking over the scene and understood exactly what she was thinking. He wished there were some way he could explain it to her. But she wouldn't understand the words even if he said them. "Don't try so hard, Maggie darling," he wanted to tell her. "It's no use. Can't you see that? We both know it. Admit it."

"It's going great, isn't it?" Cathy said as they met in the kitchen to start the coffee and whip the cream for the pies. "He fits in perfectly."

"I guess so." Maggie shook her head as she searched through the drawer for the beater attachments. "He seems to be enjoying himself. Doesn't he?"

"Sure he does." Cathy dismissed that topic with a toss of her head. "Listen, I just had the greatest idea. We ought to set Sheila up with Bill Smith. They'd make the perfect couple."

Maggie laughed. "Call him up. See if you can get him over here."

Cathy scowled. "He went up to Sacramento to spend Thanksgiving with his grandparents, from what I've heard. But I definitely will think about finding a way to throw the two of them together when he gets back."

Maggie nodded her approval. "But in the meantime, what are we going to do about Sheila?" she asked, frowning over the problem.

Destiny took a hand. Sheila, it seemed, was a chess aficionado. Maggie's father was a pretty fair chess player himself.

"I tell you what," Maggie said brightly. "You two have a nice game of chess while we"—she gestured to indicate David, Mark, Cathy and herself—"do the dishes."

"Oh, can't I help?" said Sheila.

"Oh, no," Maggie said kindly. "There's really not room for more than four in our kitchen. You just stay here and have a good time. Pamper my father."

"Why, certainly," said Sheila, eager to please Mark's father, and Maggie almost felt guilty. Almost.

Cathy gave Maggie a big grin. "Thanks, pal," she whispered as they went to the kitchen, arms laden with dirty dishes. "Now watch me go into action."

Action was hardly the word for it. For some reason Cathy's natural bubble and bounce seemed to go flat whenever Mark was around. Maggie had never noticed it before, but it was true, and this time was no exception. Other than a wry, cryptic comment now and then, Cathy hardly opened her mouth.

But Maggie couldn't concentrate on Cathy's problem right now. Her mind was full of David. David was drying dishes. The very thought was incongruous, and yet here he was, in the flesh.

"What do I do?" he asked, all innocence.

"You mean to tell me you've never dried dishes before?"

His laughing eyes surveyed the awesome task lined up before them on the counter and in the sink—the serving dishes, the gravy boats, the crystal glasses, the bone china plates, the greasy pots and pans.

"Not good dishes," he said. "I'm a paper plate man myself. And anything else I set out to drain on its own. That usually works just fine. Why don't we try it?"

"Water spots," she informed him firmly. "Besides, there wouldn't be room in the kitchen for all that draining. Here." She handed him a large dish towel.

He took it reluctantly, but he did fine on his first few attempts with the dessert plates.

"This isn't so difficult," he said, growing cocky.

"You're doing all right," Cathy said doubtfully. "But maybe you'd better leave the wineglasses to me."

The silverware was a breeze. He advanced to drying three forks at one time and began to give the others a lecture on more efficient methods of the manly art of drying.

"You've got this whole big cloth," he told them earnestly. "And yet you're just using one tiny portion of it at a time. . . ."

Elbow-deep in sudsy water, Maggie watched him, his dark head bent over the drying of a pickle dish, his brows drawn together with the effort. And as she watched, the pickle dish slid from his hands and landed with a shattering crunch on the tile floor.

Her eyes widened with shock. David looked up and met her gaze. "Oops," he said.

Suddenly they were all laughing with a near-hysteria that showed how thick the tension had been.

"That does it." Cathy snatched David's towel away. "Get him out of here. Mark and I can do this much better on our own."

Maggie hesitated. "Are you sure?"

"Absolutely. Mark will get the broken pieces up off the ground and we'll go on from there. Just get this madman out of here so we can work!"

As far as Maggie was concerned, that would kill two birds with one stone. "All right," she said quickly. "We'll take a walk." She turned to David, her eyes bright. "Would you like that? They should be putting up the Christmas lights on Main Street. We could walk down there and take a look."

Maggie put a short coat on over her gray sweater and plaid skirt, and David pulled on a cream-color cashmere sweater, and the two of them went out into the fading light of Thanksgiving evening.

The streets were deserted. Lights were coming on in the houses up and down the way. Some people had already put wreaths on their doors. The air smelled of winter and it was cold and dark, but that only gave David a good excuse to pull Maggie close against him.

"Thank you for coming," she said as they walked. "Did you have a good time?"

"I always have a good time with you."

Content, Maggie didn't notice how he'd sidestepped the question. "Did you notice Mark and Cathy? Did you know that Cathy has had a thing for Mark for years and I didn't even know it?"

He nodded. "I had a feeling there was something there."

"And you hardly know them!" She leaned her head on his shoulder, swaying with the rhythm of their matched strides. "I don't know how I could have been so blind. I'm going to have to do something to make that up to Cathy. Somehow I'm going to get the two of them together."

David grunted, and she couldn't tell if that meant approbation or skepticism. "What do you think I should do?" she asked.

"Nothing," he said bluntly.

"Oh, no, I have to help Cathy—"

"Why? People are better off left alone. Let nature take its own course. Don't try to mold people."

He sounded very earnest, much too earnest to suit her mood, so she quickly changed the subject. "Dinner was great, wasn't it? The cranberry sauce turned out so well this year. My mother grinds the berries herself, and adds orange peel. And the turkey—did you like it that way? My father used to barbecue it outside, but then we missed all the good smells. This year my mother said, inside, in the oven, absolutely. And when she says absolutely, my father doesn't say another word." She giggled and snuggled in closer still, loving the feel of the hard, warm man who held her. "It was a wonderful dinner," she said, sighing with happiness. "But just you wait—Christmas will be even better."

A gust of wind tossed her hair in her eyes as they rounded the corner that would lead them downtown, and she didn't notice how David stiffened at her words. Everything had gone so well. She couldn't imagine a reason in the world that he might want to skip another family occasion at her house.

"Christmas," she said again, enjoying the sound of the word. "You're going to love it. We usually don't have as many people, but we always try to make sure we have some children. That way Mark can dress up as Santa Claus—oh!" She turned, her smile huge and delighted. "Maybe you could be Santa Claus this year. Would you like that? It's so much fun. To see those little eyes so wide, so excited—"

"Look, Maggie." He pulled her to the side and pointed up into the cloudless night sky. "A shooting star."

"Where?" She frowned up into the purple expanse. "I don't see it. It's not dark enough yet."

"I see it," he said softly, staring up. His voice took on a touch of desperation. "I swear to God I see it."

Maggie turned and looked into his face, struck by his tone. "David?" she said questioningly, reaching for him with a tentative hand.

He looked down at her huge blue eyes and his resolve broke. "Oh, Maggie," he muttered, taking her face in his hands and showering her with quick, hungry kisses. "Oh, Maggie, what am I going to do with you?"

"Love me," she whispered, puzzled by the note of desperation in his voice. Was it asking too much just to have him for her own for a little while?

His laugh had a savage sound. Breaking away, he took her hand and began to pull her along the street. "Let's hurry," he said. "Let's get downtown and see those lights."

The lights were spectacular. They wandered for blocks like strays lost in a marvelous fantasy land, laughing at the colorful displays, dancing in the empty street, calling greetings to the workmen who were still putting the finishing touches to the decorations. It was a fun, rollicking good time, but Maggie's joy was tainted just a little by the streak of wildness she detected in David. Something was wrong. Something in him was straining to be free. Something was making him feel caught. She had no idea what it could be, but she wanted desperately to do all she could to make everything absolutely right.

When they ran out of lights, they found themselves in the park. "Are you cold?" he asked her, and she nodded. "Hold me tight," she murmured, and he kissed her. The kiss grew. It had fire in it, a fire urged on by the wildness in David.

"Oh, Maggie," he whispered against her neck. "How did I ever come to need you so much? Why the hell can't I walk away like I should?"

His words made her cold. She knew he was going to break free eventually, that she only had him for a little while. *But not yet,* she cried inside. This was too soon.

And so she used the only weapon she was sure of, and her mouth sought his again. He groaned against her lips, his hands sliding under her sweater, pushing aside her bra until both breasts were free, and he rubbed them with the palm of his hand until her nipples were full and aching and each touch was a small electric surge of ecstasy and her legs trembled.

"I want you so badly," he said, his fingers spread between her breasts, his face buried in her hair, his body taut and tight with his agonizing need. What the hell was wrong with him? Why was he so obsessed with her? She was all wrong for him, and yet he couldn't break away.

She heard that wildness again and she was ready. "I know a place," she whispered, pulling away and taking his hand. "Follow me."

They went quickly down a grassy slope and through a huge drainage pipe, into a stand of trees that hid them from all signs of civilization. Shrugging out of her coat, she dropped it to the ground and went down upon it, pulling him with her. He pulled the sweater up to reveal her full breasts, snowy white in the moonlight, the tips a dusky rose.

"Just looking at you drives me mad," he murmured, more to himself than to her. And then he was using his tongue to urge the nipples into full peaks again, pulling at them, nipping gently but with sure demand. She tossed beneath him, thinking she would scream if he went on with it, yet wanting more, more . . .

She tugged at the ends of his sweater and found the hard, smooth expanse of his chest with the flat of her hands, holding the beat of his heart at her mercy, caressing him, stirring his senses to match her own building spiral of passion. His hand slipped beneath her skirt and tore away the thin lace panties that protected her. She quivered, waiting for his touch, and when it came, she gasped, thrusting her hips up to hold him there. He went on stroking and coaxing until she cried out, tearing at his belt, and then he plunged into the dark heart of her desire and they were racing together, driving and twisting as they took from each other and gave to each other and became one.

When it was over, Maggie cried. She did it quietly and David never knew. But tears welled in her eyes and slipped silently down her cheeks before she wiped them away. What they had just shared had been true ecstasy. She'd never had passion quite so high, so rare. But something in it had frightened her. Perhaps it was the feeling that she might never have him this way again. Perhaps it was the feeling of doom that hovered over their love affair. She loved him. But how soon would she lose him?

"Too soon," she whispered into the darkness as they pulled themselves together and prepared to go back into the world. "Much too soon."

CHAPTER TEN

The entire Youth Center looked like a carnival scene—streamers, balloons, banners, the works. The town of Wakefield had just finished celebrating the Winners' victory at the County Trials Championship.

"I'm so proud of you," Maggie said, coming up behind David as he stood watching the kids digging in to a five-foot-long ice cream sundae he'd ordered for them. She put a hand on his shoulder and wished she had the nerve to get closer—but they were in public. In the two weeks since Thanksgiving he'd worked very hard with the boys on their riding, but he'd had plenty of time to spend with her as well, and they'd used it to advantage, she thought, smiling up into his dark eyes.

"Don't be proud of me," he retorted. "Be proud of them. They did it. Every one of them did magnificently."

She nodded, loving the look of thinly concealed elation in his eyes, despite what he'd said. He was thrilled. He could barely contain himself. But she wouldn't push the point. "Especially Jed," she said instead. "Did you ever think he would end up winning the novice class?"

His grin was devilish. "I knew he would."

She laughed. "Oh, sure you did." She poked him in the ribs. "Do you maybe see a little of yourself in that boy?"

"Maybe." They both watched Jed for a moment. Ice cream was being consumed at an alarming rate, and he was seated in the midst of the crowd, the center of attention, looking very full of himself. But then he had a right to it. He'd earned it.

Jed had been angry for a while at the things David had said to him at Three Rivers. But on the day after Thanksgiving he'd come to David and asked for more help, just as David had hoped he would. And the two of them had worked long hours to get Jed ready.

As Maggie and David watched, Jed got up from the table. He said something to one of the other boys, then turned toward the exit. Suddenly Randi was there. They came face to face, talked for a moment, then Jed's arm came around Randi's shoulders and they left together, arm in arm.

"Where are they going?" Maggie asked sharply.

David shrugged. "To celebrate. Jed deserves all the celebrating he can get."

She frowned, not sure she liked his attitude. "Within limits," she muttered, moving in the kids' direction. "I think I'll go out and ask them what they—"

David took a step that put his body directly in her path. "Oh no you don't," he said firmly. "Don't take responsibility for everyone and everything that goes on in this town. For God's sake, set yourself free a little."

She hesitated, searching his dark gaze. Maybe he was right. Maybe less involvement *was* freedom. He ought to know. Before he'd come to Wakefield he'd been a master at it. Maybe she ought to try it for once.

"All right," she said grudgingly, settling back against the rail. "But I don't think Randi's parents would like it if they knew she and Jed were seeing each other."

"Let them complain, then, and do something about it themselves. It's not our problem."

"No?"

"No."

His arm came around her and she sighed, resting her head on his shoulder. She would try it his way for once. After all, she had problems of her own.

Later that evening Maggie and David were in bed. They'd just made slow, sweet love and the afterglow was still with them. David stroked her golden hair and stared into the shadows of his bedroom.

"Are you tired?" she asked softly, sensing he was brooding.

"A little."

"Do you want me to stay tonight?"

He hesitated, sending a sliver of ice through her heart, but finally he said, "Of course. I always want you to stay."

Relieved, she turned, molding her body to his. "Good. I want to stay. I'm still high from all the excitement. I don't want to be alone."

She didn't try to analyze why she felt the need to cling to him tonight. After all, things were going well, she thought, closing her eyes as his fingers stroked her neck. The boys had done much better than expected at the championships. That could mean only good things—for the boys and for herself. David had to see now how much he meant to the community. Now that he'd had this heady taste of success with the boys, surely he would want more. He would be eager to start a new program, maybe get into more of the activities at the Youth Center. And the more involved he got, the less he would think about leaving. . . . She sighed, turning so that David's magic hands could find more of her to caress. She could feel he was uneasy, unsettled, tonight. But she wouldn't question him. She would close her eyes and pretend everything was perfect.

David's eyes were wide open, staring into the darkness. More than uneasiness was rushing through his blood. *What the hell am I going to do?* he was thinking. *I'm getting trapped. I'm in the middle of a great big trap. Maggie was the bait, and I walked in, because I couldn't resist the temptation. Now the jaws of the trap are closing down on me. I've got to get out of here before it's too late.*

But how could he go? His hands pulled back the sheet and his fingers found her breast, teased the swollen nipple. She was too important to him now, too much an integral part of his life. What would he do without her warm body, her sweet smile? He'd never cared for another woman the way he cared for her, never wanted another woman over and over again the way he did her. He pushed back the rest of the sheet and took in the wealth he held before him—the full, rounded hips, the smooth thighs, the beautiful breasts—and desire uncurled inside him again.

"Maggie," he whispered huskily.

She didn't even open her eyes. Stretching her naked body in front of him, she smiled and reached out to touch him, knowing unerringly where to put her warm hand.

"I love you, David," she whispered, so low he hardly heard it, but he'd known it for weeks. And as he made love to her, the sort of love he'd never dreamed in the old days that he might be capable of, he thought it too: *I love you.*

They'd barely finished when the banging started on the front door. "Duke! You in there?"

Maggie shot up in the bed, pulling the sheet around her.

"Who is it?" David called out, rolling out of bed and stumbling toward the light.

"It's Burt. This is important. Open up."

"Just a minute." David quickly pulled on his slacks and Maggie reached for her clothes, putting them on with shaking fingers.

David had the door open before Maggie came out of the bedroom. "Hi there, Burt. What's up?"

Burt entered, looking worried. "We've got problems, David, serious problems." Then his gaze fell on Maggie coming out of the bedroom and his jaw dropped. "Oh," he said weakly.

David had no patience with Burt's shattered illusions. "What is it?" he asked, his voice brusque.

Burt stared at Maggie for a moment longer, his face full of concern. It took an effort for him to return his attention to David.

"Problems, as I said." He gathered himself together. "Mr. Farlow—you know who he is?"

David nodded. "Of course. He's the major stockholder in Farlow Electronics and most of the rest of the industry in this town."

Burt nodded. "He's also the major benefactor of the Youth Center. And his wife heads the fund-raising committee."

"And he's Randi Farlow's father," Maggie chimed in, somehow sensing where the discussion was going.

"Exactly." Burt pulled out a handkerchief and wiped his brow. "Well, he got wind of the fact that his daughter has been seeing the Jed Marker boy, and he forbade her to see him again. Well, you know what Randi's like—you want her to do something, you just forbid her to do it. That's the surest way to get what you want."

"So?" For some reason David had gone very cold.

"So they ran away together, Randi and Jed."

"I don't believe it!" Maggie gasped, even as she recalled the picture the two of them had made leaving the Youth Center arm in arm. Immediately she felt responsible. "How did this happen?"

David took a firm grip on her wrist to quiet her. "What else?" he asked, quietly intense. "Let's have it."

"She went out her bedroom window about an hour ago. They drove off on one of the motorcycles I got for the kids. As you can imagine, Mr. Farlow is fit to be tied."

David shook his head, a humorless smile on his dark face. "Damn," was all he said.

"The thing is, Mr. Farlow is holding us accountable." Burt wiped his forehead again, looking from one to the other of them as though he half-expected them to be angry with him too. "They met at the Youth Center, they rode off on our bike—"

"Did Farlow call the police?"

"Sure."

"See if you can hold them off for a while. I think I know where the kids went. Jed's told me about this special place of his down near Porterville where he wanted to try some riding. I'll make a run down there and see if I can find them."

"Oh, good." Burt was relieved to find someone who had an idea of something to do. "What'll I tell Mr. Farlow? He's over at the Youth Center and he's hopping mad."

"I'll go back with you," Maggie said. "Let me get my coat."

"Good luck," she said to David as he left.

He turned back and touched her cheek with his finger. "Hope you're up to date on your tetanus shots," he said without much humor. "Farlow's got a bite to go with that nasty bark of his."

"I'll be careful," she said, trying to smile.

"You'd better be." He dropped a quick kiss on her lips and strode out the door. In a moment she could hear his motorcycle roaring off down the street.

They rode back to the Youth Center in Burt's car. All the way there the silence was thick enough to cut.

Mr. Farlow was at their throats before they made it through the doorway. A small, white-haired man, he had the aggressive qualities of a bull terrier, and he kind of looked like one as well.

"Where's my daughter?" he demanded, striding toward Maggie. "You were in charge of my daughter's welfare, Maggie Jones. Now see what's happened? Not a very good protector of your young charges, are you? If you let this sort of hanky-panky go on right underneath your nose—"

"Calm down, Mr. Farlow," Maggie said quietly. "Yelling at me isn't going to solve anything."

That only made him more angry. "Do you think you're going to get away with this incompetence?" he cried. "I'll have your job for this. You and that motorcycle hoodlum, that David Duke. You'll both pay—"

"Mr. Farlow." Maggie's tone had hardened to cold fury. "David Duke is out right now trying to find your daughter. He'll bring her back safe and sound. Now if you'll excuse me, I'm going to make some telephone calls to some of Randi's friends to see if they have any idea where she might be."

She did just that until almost midnight, dialing one number after another. Randi had a lot of friends, but Maggie had no luck at all. And Mr. Farlow appeared in the doorway to her office periodically to issue more threats regarding her job, her career, even her family life.

"I've had it," she told Burt at last. "Can you give me a ride home?"

"Home?" he said hopefully.

She felt herself flushing. "I really mean back to David's."

But he smiled. "Sure," he said in his kindly manner.

Once she got to David's apartment, she wandered around the lonely rooms like a lost soul. There was a heavy lump in the pit of her stomach, and a feeling of doom hung in the air. She'd never been there without David before. The rooms seemed hollow. Like her life would be without him.

And yet with just her memories of the last few weeks they'd spent together, she could people the rooms again. She remembered the pillow fight they'd had in the bedroom, the time in the kitchen when he'd made pancakes for her and they'd stuck to the pan, the showers in the bathroom, the time he'd soaped her down from the top of her head to the tips of her toes . . .

The memories would be part of her always. No one could take them away. Whenever she thought of them, she would smile and feel warm again.

She shook herself. Why was she acting as though things were over already? David wasn't going anywhere. There were three months to go on his contract, and she meant to enjoy them—and use every minute to work on convincing him not to go at all.

She dozed on the couch, half-listening to hear David's key in the lock. When it finally came, she jumped up, blinking groggily.

He came in slowly, glanced at her, then shrugged out of his jacket. She couldn't read a thing in his impassive face.

"Well, come on," she urged. "What happened?"

"I found them." He pulled off his leather gloves and flung them down on the table. "I got them to come back with me."

She frowned at him, still misty with sleep and not sure she was reading his mood quite right. He should have been happier, prouder. She wanted to run up and hold him, throw her arms around his neck, but some signal he was sending held her back. He had a "don't tread on me" shield up. A quiver of unease snaked through her.

"How did you manage to do that?" she asked, sinking back down onto the sofa.

"I convinced them it would be better for me to bring them back than to wait for the police to catch up with them." He lowered his tired body down on the sofa, but not close to her. "They saw the logic in my argument and came along quietly." He grimaced, stretching out his long legs before him. "They were already cold and hungry, and they'd just started to realize that without any money they weren't going to get very far."

"So you brought them back." The air was curiously dead between them. "What did Mr. Farlow say?"

David turned his face and stared at her, his huge black eyes hard as obsidian. "He fired me."

"What?" She went numb. Of course. Why hadn't she thought of that? It had never even occurred to her. When he'd threatened to fire them both, she'd only considered their jobs at the Youth Center. But David worked for Farlow Electronics. "He didn't! He can't! You're on contract—"

"He holds the contract. He can break it at will."

Maggie drew her legs up under her. "We'll fight it," she said, her eyes fiery. "I'll go to him and tell him just exactly what he can do with—"

"No you won't." David moved closer and took her hand in his. "Just leave things alone, Maggie."

"Oh well," she said shakily, running a hand through her hair. "We'll find you something else. There are hundreds of jobs for computer programmers. Or . . . listen, Mark has always wanted to quit and form his own consulting firm, if he could only find the right man to go in with. We'll talk to him, get his ideas—"

"No, we won't." He took her chin in his hand. "Maggie, try to understand. I'm glad Farlow fired me. I want to get out of here."

Everything seemed to go white around her. All she could see was David's face. "What do you mean?" she whispered.

"I told you from the first that I never stay anywhere very long. Some places I can stand longer than others. But this place . . . Maggie, it's crowding me. I've got to go."

"Go?" Her throat was so dry, she could hardly talk. "But you're not finished here. What—what about your work at the Youth Center?"

He shrugged. "It was fun, but it's not what I want to do with my time, my life. There's a big world out there, Maggie. I want to see all of it."

The room was spinning, and she felt as though she were struggling for air. "What about . . ." She couldn't even bring herself to say it. *What about us?*

After all, he'd told her from the very beginning that there was no "us." How could she throw it in his face now? She turned away so that he wouldn't see the knife in her heart. "Where will you go?" she asked, her voice strained. "Rio? Saudia Arabia?"

"Not yet. I've heard about a temporary opening in Los Angeles I thought I'd look into. That will give me time to decide where I want to jump to next." He moved restlessly. "A small editing company wants to computerize. I figure I can help them set up the software to do it. I'll give them a call in the morning."

She turned back, staring at him. "You've been planning this for a long time," she accused, feeling betrayed.

He reached for her, but she pulled away. "In a way, Maggie, I was," he admitted. "I'm sorry, I'm so sorry. But I'm not your small-town boy. I never can be."

"But you can!" she cried. "You've done so well here. Everybody loves you. And your work with the Winners . . ." She shook her head, trying to shake out the fuzzy cobwebs. "You'll miss it," she insisted. "The community service—"

"Are you nuts?" He laughed harshly. "Sure, it was fun. But look what it got me: fired from my job. It's better to stay free of entanglements. You get into less trouble that way."

She swallowed. "You enjoyed the Thanksgiving dinner with my parents," she said stubbornly.

"It was all right, sure." He knew he had to be brutally honest with her. There was no other way. He put his hands on her shoulders to force her to listen. "But you want to know what? All the time it reminded me of being caught in a spider's web, with all the little sticky strands out there trying to tie me down and hold me in place. That's what a small town is like. That's what families are like. I can live without it." He almost shook her, so determined was he to get his point across. "I can soar without it. With it, I'm tied to the ground. Don't you see?"

She saw and knew that it was hopeless. He wouldn't be argued into staying, no matter what she said. Her heart twisted with pain and she turned away from him, rising from the sofa and stumbling across the room.

He was right behind her, stopping her with a hand on her arm. "I have just one other thing to add, Maggie." He paused, then went ahead, recklessly. "Do you want to come with me?"

She whirled and stared at him. The room was spinning even more crazily now. What was he asking?

"Come with me." He drew her into his arms and held her close. "I'm not talking marriage, I'm not talking a long-term commitment, I'm talking here and now. You know that. But I can't stand the thought of being without you, Maggie. Will you come with me?"

"To Los Angeles?"

"That's where I'm headed."

"For how long?"

"For as long as we still want to be together."

That would be always in her case, there wasn't a doubt in her mind. Didn't he know that?

"For as long as we both still want the arrangement." He wanted to be perfectly clear.

Arrangement. She felt ill. An arrangement of convenience. Something shriveled inside her and she turned to look out the window at the streetlights that lit up the purple night sky. The lights of her town, Wakefield. Her parents, her brother, her friends, her boss—all the people who had loved and cared for her all her life. The people who had made her what she was. The people whose lives had been changed just through knowing her. Could she leave them? Could she leave it all behind and go with a man who wasn't even offering her marriage?

"I—I don't know," she stammered. She couldn't even think straight. "I don't know what to say."

He took her in his arms again. "Don't think," he ordered fiercely. "You're coming with me. I need you." His mouth took hers in a kiss that reinforced his words. "Oh Maggie, Maggie, I need you so." His face nuzzled into the hollow behind her ear. "Come with me. It won't be forever. You can always come back when you're ready to. The town will still be here."

Come back? When he was tired of her? And what condition would she be in when she returned? How could she tell her parents? They'd always assumed she would be nearby all their lives. How could she tell Mark, Burt, Cathy?

And yet she melted in his arms. How could she resist what her heart wanted anyway? Home . . . or David? "All right," she whispered against his strong chest. "I'll go with you."

"Oh Maggie, darling Maggie." He covered her face with kisses. "We'll have such a good time together. I can hardly wait to take you to some of the fabulous nightspots in Los Angeles. We'll have a whole world to explore. We'll really broaden your horizons."

"I don't want my horizons broadened," she murmured, clinging to him. "I just want you."

"Maggie, you won't regret it. I'll make sure you don't."

How could he promise that when she already regretted it?

Grow up, Maggie Jones, she shouted silently at herself. *People leave their hometowns every day. You can do it too.*

They went to bed and he held her and stroked her hair and she smiled up at him and told him how happy she was. But it was a lie.

She'd never been more unhappy in her life. How could she choose between her home and the man she loved? She almost hated him for making her do it.

She kept up the smile until she thought that he'd gone to sleep, and then she cried.

But David wasn't asleep. He lay very still and made his breathing even, but his dark eyes were wide open and he heard every sob, could visualize every tear that slipped down her face. And he did hate himself.

What the hell was he doing to her? What had happened to him? How had he suddenly gone so weak? He'd messed up her life just by being in it. David Duke, the man who claimed he didn't want to make a difference in anyone's life. He'd ruined hers. And if he took her along with him, he would only go on ruining it.

How could he take her away from her family and everything she loved? She might not hold it against him at first, but eventually she couldn't help but resent it. And the longer he kept her away, the more she would grow to detest him for it.

He'd asked her to come along with him because he was too selfish to lose her. He'd claimed it was to spare her pain, but he was only kidding himself. What was this if not pain? And how bad would the pain be when they decided to separate at last? No, it would be far kinder to leave her now, make a clean break. Anything else was only prolonging her agony. It would be doing her a favor to go ahead and leave without her.

She seemed to have fallen asleep at last.

"Maggie?" he whispered.

She didn't stir. He slid out of the bed and began to pull his things together. It didn't take long to pack. He didn't have much, just what he could shove into a duffel bag and one flat suitcase. He stopped in the kitchen to write her a note, and then he was gone, heading for Los Angeles, leaving Wakefield, and feeling like a murderer escaping the scene of the crime.

CHAPTER ELEVEN

It didn't take Maggie long to get over the worst of her sorrow. Why, within a week she didn't cry any longer when she heard David's name. Within days she didn't feel as though she couldn't breathe when she thought of his dark eyes. She was strong. She'd done just fine before he'd ever arrived in Wakefield. She'd do just fine now that he was gone.

Luckily it was a very busy time of year, and she was so full of plans and projects that she hardly had time to think of her problems. Christmas was just weeks away. And then it was just days away. The Youth Center was putting on a pageant, and Maggie was in charge.

"Would you like me to find someone else to handle it?" Burt had asked her hesitantly. He hadn't come right out and said "I told you so," for which she was grateful, but he cared for her and he knew how it hurt.

"Are you kidding?" She'd perfected the breezy attitude —it covered a multitude of heartaches. "Don't you dare let anyone else near it. It's my baby."

No, the worst of the pain had been in those first few weeks. She was getting better now. She only thought of

David once or twice every ten minutes now. Someday she was going to bring that down to once an hour.

Christmas was upon them, and the streets were full of shoppers hurrying home with armloads of gaily wrapped packages. Snow had fallen in the mountains. Carols rang out from every store doorway. It was usually Maggie's favorite time of year.

She'd done most of her Christmas shopping already, resisting the urge to buy things for David at every turn. Today, sitting in her office, she closed her eyes and thought of what to get her brother for Christmas. And when she opened her eyes she found herself staring straight at the African violet David had given her. The flowers were dead now, little blackened stalks. "Overwatering," someone had said. "You can't smother them with affection, you know."

"Did I smother you, David?" she whispered.

It was a bleak, gray day, and her spirits sank.

"Oh, by the way," Burt said as he passed her office. "I just heard that Randi Farlow is being sent away to a boarding school. You're going to have to find yourself a new gymnastics star."

Poor Randi. She tapped her pencil against her blotter and thought of the two children who'd dreamed of being lovers. Would they get together next summer? In later years? Probably not. Randi would change. Jed would find another girl. How sad.

A picture of Cathy's unhappy face sprang into her mind, too. Mark was still dating Sheila. He'd just been promoted at Farlow and had been talking obliquely about how he needed a wife. Maggie groaned. Didn't love ever go right? Slowly, deliberately, she picked up the little African violet plant and dumped it in her trash can.

She stayed late that night to work on some proposals for next year. Working was better than pining at home. It was almost ten o'clock when her telephone rang and she found a frantic Cathy on the other end.

"Maggie? Oh, thank God I found you. Can you come quick? I'm only allowed one phone call, and—"

"Cathy, where are you?"

"I've been arrested! Can you come?"

Of course she could come. She jumped into her little car and raced toward the police station, the possibilities whirring through her mind. What on earth could Cathy have been arrested for? Doing one of her can-can dances? Running a red light?

"Breaking and entering," the sergeant read off sternly. "She was caught burglarizing the apartment of one Mark Jones of Dunsmore Way."

Maggie felt as though she'd entered the twilight zone. "May I see her?"

"Sure. Come this way."

The room was bare except for a table and two chairs. Maggie thought she'd never seen Cathy looking so frightened.

"What on earth is going on here?" Maggie cried, throwing her arms around her shivering friend and hugging her tightly. "What were you doing?"

Tears trembled in Cathy's eyes. "I was . . . I was just . . . Oh, Maggie, this is so awful! Mark is going to kill me. They're going to throw me in jail!"

"Tell me." She settled Cathy back down in her chair

and pulled the other chair over closer, sitting in it herself. "Start at the beginning."

"I just wanted to help celebrate Mark's promotion." Her eyes were huge, like a puppy's. Maggie's heart went out to her. "I thought I'd decorate his apartment while he was gone. I knew he was taking Sheila to the movies, so I took a ladder over and put it up against the wall of his building. But I let it go a little too soon, and it broke a window."

"Oh, Cathy."

She nodded sadly. "Yes, I know, I felt awful. Why does everything I do always turn out wrong? But I went on, climbing up with my backpack full of streamers and party hats and things I was going to use to surprise him when he got home. Only someone heard the window break and called the cops, and when they got there, they wouldn't even listen to me. I mean, I had all that stuff. Do they really think I was going to steal everything Mark owns and then leave streamers behind?"

It seemed they did think that. The stern sergeant came in again and he wasn't pleasant. Then, suddenly, Mark burst into the room. "Cathy?" he said as though he couldn't believe his eyes. "What the hell are you doing here?"

Cathy turned to Maggie, despair written on her face. "Oh, get me out of here," she said with a groan. "He'll never forgive me for this."

But Mark had turned on the police officer. "What do you think you're doing?" he demanded. "This is a friend of mine. She had every right to be in my apartment."

"I don't think you understand, buddy. The little lady broke a window—"

"I understand perfectly." He swung around, and when he found Cathy crying, he was beside her in an instant and his arms were around her, protective, soothing. "No charges," he said gruffly. Cathy's head tipped up so that she could look into his face.

"You aren't mad?" she whispered, a little girl again.

He tousled her hair. "I'm not mad," he said, his voice husky with something that sounded almost like affection. He glanced coldly at the policeman again. "I'll take her home now, if you have no further objections."

Maggie watched in amazement, then followed the two of them out to the parking lot. Mark settled Cathy into the passenger seat and then came around the car, where Maggie stopped him.

"Mark," she said, "what's going on?"

"Nothing," he said gruffly. "I'll take care of Cathy. See you tomorrow."

And he slid behind the wheel and started the car's engine. As they drove off, Maggie saw Cathy's bewildered face peering back at her through the midnight gloom. And she began to laugh.

When the laughter was done, Maggie went slowly back to her own apartment. Cathy and Mark. There was a lesson to be learned here, she kept telling herself. If only she could figure out what it was.

The question kept her awake most of the night. It was almost dawn when she decided she knew the answer. If you loved someone, you didn't give up. Like Cathy, you kept trying, no matter how much it hurt.

"No matter how much it hurts," she repeated out loud, and then she went to sleep.

She went into the office the next morning, not to work but to retrieve the African violet from the trash before it was too late.

"I'm going down to Los Angeles," she told Burt abruptly. "I'm sorry, I guess you'll have to get someone else to cover the pageant after all. I'm going to look for David."

"Maggie." His eyes were full of worry. "Do you think you should?"

She patted his cheek. "Burt, I know I should. I'm only sorry to leave you in the lurch."

"But your parents . . . Christmas . . ."

"Everyone will do just fine without me," she said firmly. "I'll miss Christmas, but it won't kill me."

She went home and packed a few things, then called the airport. The next flight south was leaving in two hours. That gave her time to call her parents and still get to the airport on time.

"I can't say that I'm surprised," her mother said gently. "I was wondering why you let him go so easily."

"I was insane." Maggie's voice was choked. "But I'm over that now. Save some holly for me."

"Oh, darling, we will. Just do what you have to do. And good luck."

The drive to the airport seemed to last forever. She kept thinking of things she hadn't done, people she hadn't called, but it was too late now. She was on her way.

She planned to fly into Burbank and get a room in a

hotel. David had left the name of the editing company he thought he'd probably work for. She only prayed he'd gotten the job, because if he hadn't, she had no idea how she would find him.

"I can't really fly down to Rio and look around, can I?" she whispered to herself. And David, the drifter, would leave few clues behind.

The airport was packed with people, everyone bundled up warmly and carrying packages. Maggie pushed her way to the Intrastate Airline counter and asked for her ticket.

"Would you like to check any luggage?"

"No, thanks. I'll carry it on."

She smiled, thinking she was getting as independent as David. *Have small carry-on luggage, will travel,* she thought with a grin. Her heart fluttered. She was excited. She knew without a doubt that this was the right thing to do.

The holiday crowds were thickening fast. She managed to find a chair and she sat still, holding on to the quiver of excitement she'd had ever since she'd made her decision, refusing to consider all the bad things that might go wrong with her plans. Flight after flight was called, and the crowd grew more and more packed, and then there it was, flight 502 to Burbank and San Diego, now loading at Gate 1A.

She had to push her way into the line heading toward Gate 1A. *Good lord,* she thought, wincing as someone's suitcase hit her knee, *this could get dangerous.* She'd never been in a place that was so crowded before, and for just a minute she had a flutter of panic, wondering if she was going to be able to make it to the gate in time.

The mob all around her was noisy, but suddenly a voice cut through the din. It was a sound she recognized, but she couldn't quite make it out. She looked around, then shrugged and put her shoulder to the mass exit once again.

"Maggie!"

There it was again. She turned and stared around this way and that through the crowd. That voice . . .

"Maggie! Up here!"

"Come on, lady," a much less pleasant voice hissed in her ear at the same time. "Move it. I'll miss my plane."

She tried to move out of the man's way, but it was impossible. The mob was packing in closer all the time and she was being pushed along with the flow of it toward the boarding ramp.

"Maggie!"

She lifted her gaze to the escalators, and then she saw him. He was at the top of a stalled escalator, in as miserable a crowd as she was.

"David!" she cried, hardly believing her eyes.

"Watch it, lady!" Others bumped against her but she stood staring back, her gaze glued to the figure at the top of the escalator. What was he doing here?

"Wait for me!" he called to her.

But she couldn't stop. The crowd was surging around her, carrying her along with it.

"I can't!" she called back, but she began to fight the current, adrenaline rushing through her veins. Why was he here? What could it mean? There was only one thing to do. She had to get to him and find out.

It wasn't easy. In the course of her struggle she was cursed at, scratched, and she lost the carry-on luggage she'd been so proud of.

"My shoe!" she cried as the low-heeled pump slipped off and disappeared into the raging torrent of humanity. But what did it matter? At last, beside a marble pillar that afforded them at least partial protection from the zoo around them, they found each other.

For just a moment their gazes locked and the world around them fell away. She searched his face hungrily, and he did the same with hers. He didn't smile, and neither did she. Now that they were face to face, she wasn't sure . . .

"What are you doing here?" she asked shyly. He looked so wonderful.

His dark eyes wavered, and his gaze dropped to stare at her hands, held so tightly in front of her to keep her from reaching for him. His face looked hard, almost cold.

"I just arrived," he said casually. "Flew in to—wrap up some old business." His gaze rose quickly, as though he hoped to catch something in her face.

"Oh." Did he hear the disappointment in her voice? For just a second she'd allowed herself to hope. But no, he was here on business. "I—I'm glad we ran into each other. I'm on my way out." She gestured vaguely toward the loading areas.

"Oh?" He jammed his hand into his pocket and shifted his weight. "Where are you going?"

Nowhere, now. Was that a lump she felt in her throat? She smiled brightly, trying to ignore it. "Los Angeles."

He frowned. "What for?"

"To visit an old friend." She thought of the ticket in her handbag. It was useless now.

"I see." He tried to grin. "We were old friends once."

"I know."

His dark eyes penetrated her brittle disguise. "Do you hate me, Maggie?" he asked softly.

She shook her head. Her face felt stiff and awkward. "I may hate what you did," she said evenly, "but I could never hate you."

He searched her face as though waiting for something else. She avoided his eyes. What more could she give him? He knew how she loved him, didn't he? And if this was all he wanted to do about it, what was she doing here?

Was there nothing else to say? The silence grew strained. "I guess I'd better get to my plane," Maggie said at last, then wanted to bite her tongue. What was she, crazy? If she kept this up, she would find herself on an airplane to Los Angeles, making a trip to nowhere for nothing.

He moved uncomfortably. "Yeah. I've got to go look for a taxicab."

Their gazes met. Something quivered between them, and Maggie held her breath. Was he going to speak? She waited, lips parted, and he scowled and shook his head. He turned away with a wrenching movement.

"Have a good time in L.A.," he said huskily.

"I will," she whispered, watching him start to merge

back into the moving crowd. Her eyes stung and she closed them, turning around, her back to him. Was it really so dead, what had been between them? Was it over?

"Maggie!"

She swung around again. He was coming back.

"David!"

"Maggie, I—damn it!"

Suddenly his arms were around her and he was pulling her close.

"I can't help it, Maggie," he whispered roughly. "I just can't stay away from you."

"David," she whispered, and then her voice choked with tears.

"Darling, darling," he murmured, and he held her to him tightly, as though to make up for all the wasted days when he hadn't been able to hold her at all.

She leaned back, the tears shimmering in her eyes, but her mouth turned up in a smile. "Let me look at you," she said shakily, leaning back even farther for a better view.

David's tie was askew, but for the rest he looked in much better shape than she. "Oh Maggie, darling," he said with a laugh once he got a good look at her. "You're a mess!"

She touched his face, his collar, his suitcoat.

He touched her cheek, and there was something almost vulnerable about his look. "I—I thought I'd come home for Christmas," he said softly, his eyes dark, fathomless. "Am I welcome?"

"Welcome?" She was overwhelmed. "But I thought you hated—"

He pulled her closer and rocked her in his arms. "I hated being away from you," he told her harshly. "That was what I hated most of all. So I came back to try again, if—if you'll let me."

She tried to laugh but it came out like a hiccup. "I was just on my way down to Los Angeles to get you," she said, her voice uneven.

"You were ready to give up your Christmas to come looking for me?" He felt choked with emotion himself. To cover it he swept her back into his arms.

"We've got to go someplace to talk," he said. They looked out at the crowd. It showed no signs of lessening. Trying to make it to the exit alive would be running the gauntlet.

"Let's stay until the crowd dies down," she suggested. "We can talk here."

David looked around them and grinned. "What a madhouse. But then, maybe that's where a discussion like this belongs." He took her chin in his hand. "I had to come back to you, Maggie," he told her simply. "Any way you want it, that's how it will be. There's nothing for me out there without you."

She hesitated. "In your note you said—"

"Forget the note. I was demented that night. I've been demented for ages."

"No, David—"

"Yes. I had a chance to do a lot of soul searching. I've been an idiot. I'd built myself this stupid macho sort of self-image where I didn't need anyone else and I wouldn't let anyone else need me. Then I ran into you, Maggie Jones, and it was like running into a brick wall, and I was walking around in a daze ever after. I've finally woken from my stupor and seen the light." He kissed her softly on the lips. "I had to go away to realize what you mean to me. I had to learn what real misery was to realize you were the cure. You are where it's at, lovely lady. And that's where I want to be."

Finally she got a word in edgewise. "But I was the one who was wrong, David."

"No—"

"Yes." She took hold of his lapels and spoke earnestly. "I was acting like a baby, trying to cling to everything I was used to and have you, too. I realize now that it's time I went out into the world, like you said. I don't always have to stay in the same place. It will be good for me to see what life is like out there."

He pulled her close to him, chuckling. "That's true for a lot of people, Maggie," he told her lovingly. "But not for you. You belong to Wakefield. And it belongs to you. You love this town, you're part of the pulse of it. For most people any town, any city will do. But not for you. You belong here. And I'm going to do my damnedest to like it."

"You are?"

"I am."

"But you said you felt trapped here."

"And I was telling the truth when I said that. But I was refusing to grow up myself. It was life that was closing in on me, and I was scared to face it. I didn't know if I could cut it, so I ran away instead."

Maggie couldn't imagine David scared of anything. "And now?"

"And now I'm ready to face the music." He took her in his arms and turned her as though they were in the middle of a dance floor. "I don't promise to be perfect. You know how I am. I'm quick-tempered, rough—and I don't know a thing about families. But I want to learn. Maggie, you'll have to teach me."

They held each other, turning around and around in the midst of the airport until they were both dizzy and ready to drop.

"But wait a minute," Maggie said suddenly. "Your job in L.A.—"

He shook his head. "Couldn't keep my mind on it."

"Your motorcycles—"

"I was in such a rush to get to you, I left them behind. I'll have them shipped up eventually. Maggie . . ." He held her face in his hands and stared down at her, his expression serious. "You understand, don't you? I don't know if this will work. I only know I can't stand living without you. And for that I'm willing to try anything."

She nodded. "So am I," she whispered. "Oh, so am I!" She smiled up at him, all her love in her eyes. A voice suddenly cracked the bubble of personal space they'd created around themselves. "Excuse me. Miss?" It was a skycap with her carry-on luggage in his hand. "Is this yours?"

She looked around, slightly dazed. The airport had emptied out and they hadn't even noticed. "Y-yes, thank you." She reached out to take it, but there was more.

The skycap held out a slightly bruised shoe. "And is this yours, too?" he asked, his gaze traveling between the two of them and back down to her bare foot with uncontained curiosity.

"Yes, thank you," she said with as much dignity as she could muster, taking it grandly and putting it back on. "I guess we might as well go," she told David, suppressing her laughter. The skycap watched them as they walked slowly, arm in arm, from the terminal.

"I've got my car here," she said. "Shall we go back to my place?"

He nuzzled her neck. "Yes, and in a hurry. It's been a long time, you know."

They walked down the ramp and into the parking lot. She sighed, snuggling against him. His large, hard body was hers. Would she be able to make him happy? If not, it wouldn't be for lack of trying!

They got into her car and he leaned across to hold her one more time. His kiss was hot, and she could feel the current of passion running strong in him.

"Hey, mister," she murmured breathlessly. "Wait a minute. We're almost home."

"I don't know if I can wait." His words were teasing but his tone was serious. "Come on, darling. Let's hurry. I've been dreaming of this for weeks."

"Me too." She sighed as his arms pulled away. They would have to wait a few minutes, but that wasn't much, now that they had their whole life before them. "Me too," she whispered again as the car sped down the freeway toward her apartment. His eyes met hers in the light of the oncoming cars. The smile they shared said it all. They had a love to last a lifetime.